T0194884

OTHER BOOKS BY JIM MORTENSEN

Non Fiction:

Fiction:

Railroad (Double) Crossing:

A novel

A Skirmish in the Lionel vs MTH Train War

JIM MORTENSEN

iUniverse, Inc.
New York   Bloomington

Railroad (Double) Crossing: A novel
A Skirmish in the Lionel vs MTH Train War

This is a work of fiction. All of the characters, names, incidents, organizations, and dialogue
in this novel are either the products of the author's imagination or are used fictitiously.

iUniverse books may be ordered through booksellers or by contacting:

iUniverse
1663 Liberty Drive
Bloomington, IN 47403
www.iuniverse.com
1-800-Authors (1-800-288-4677)

Because of the dynamic nature of the Internet, any Web addresses or links contained in this book
may have changed since publication and may no longer be valid. The views expressed in this work
are solely those of the author and do not necessarily reflect the views of the publisher, and the
publisher hereby disclaims any responsibility for them.

ISBN: 978-1-4502-0120-9 (pbk)
ISBN: 978-1-4502-0117-9 (cloth)
ISBN: 978-1-4502-0118-6 (ebook)

Printed in the United States of America

iUniverse rev. date:01/19/10

— Dedication —

I would like to dedicate this book to my parents, Herchel and Catharine Mortensen, who, back in 1946, gave me my first Lionel train set. If I had only had the foresight to have kept it, it would be worth a fortune today. Additional, I would like to add to this dedication all those moms and dads who still buy their children electric trains and help to continue this wonderful hobby in spite of the fact that most no longer are familiar with the golden age of the railroads.

— Acknowledgments —

Once again I have to thank my wife, Karen, for all her editing help on the manuscript, I'm sure she was bored rereading my constant changes and finding errors to be corrected. Again too, I have to caution that because I can never really leave the manuscript alone after she finds my mistakes, any errors that have crept in after she finished are entirely my fault. Also, thanks to both of my daughters for reading through one or the other of the versions of this book and making suggestions as well as Joan Swertfager for her encouragement. Finally, I have to give a big "Thank You" to Allen Miller and Marty FitzHenry for volunteering to look over the manuscript and correcting me on the history of electric toy trains in general and the MTH/Lionel connections in particular. Any mistakes in this regard are mine, not theirs.

— Preface —

As the twentieth century turned to the twenty-first, there was a civil war raging in the toy train hobby between those who ran and/or collected O-gauge toy trains. The icon of the hobby, Lionel LLC, was being challenged by an upstart company, Mike's Train House (MTH), for the minds, hearts and pocketbooks of those in the hobby or just beginning in it. This was a war being fought by more disinformation, innuendo, or out-right lies than either of the 2000 or 2004 political campaigns. This misinformation was being spread primarily through the Internet chat rooms, web sites or blogs that sprung up and were being manned by enthusiasts favoring one side or the other. Often the commentary was venomous, even treating and certainly questioning their opponents' manhood. Like any civil war, it demonized the heads of the rival companies; pitted friend against friend; brother against brother; father against son. The skirmishes and battles of this war would be fought out in some of the darnedest places and in the strangest of ways.

One of these places would be upstate New York's Palatine County. Palatine County is the second smallest county—after New York County, aka Manhattan—in the state. Unlike the smaller one this means that unless you live there, or better still, have moved away from there, you probably know little about it. Palatine County is located in the western foothills of the Catskill Mountains. This in itself is a misnomer since these are not really mountains at all, but the northern part of the Appalachian Chain and are actually remnants of a plateau. What are known as "mountains" are actually what is left after this plateau, having been pushed up from an ancient sea floor, was glaciated and eroded into a series of hills and valleys—the latter known locally as "cloves". The area, once heavily forested, had been considered by the Indians to be so inhospitable for most of the year that no tribe claimed or settled there but rather used it for summer hunting and a vacation area—much like the New York City residents who would centuries later flock to Grossinger's and Hunter Mountain in the same area. Given the background of the residents and their economic conditions, this area was hardly a place one would suspect to find electric train enthusiasts much less the site of a life and death battle.

First of all, there was a genetic thing; over half the residents were descended from the original settlers who were not, nor ever would be, frivolous people. These first Caucasian residents were escapees from a group of settlers sent over by order of Queen Anne in the 1700's to alleviate crowding and rid England of refugees from Roman Catholic persecution. Lest their particular brand of Lutheranism cause religious unrest in other segments of her population, Her Majesty handed over their care and resettlement to Robert Livingston. Her only requirement from Livingston was for him to make good use of them, preferably in some service to the Crown. The émigrés, who were originally from the Palatine region of Germany—thus the name later given to the county—were given passage to Livingston's Hudson River holdings in the New World in exchange for the lifetime service of producing stores of pine pitch and rosin for the Royal Navy. Disembarked on both sides of the river in the middle of the river's valley, these settlers—referred to as "Dutchmen" only because they spoke Deutsch and had a short hiatus in Holland prior to landing in England—immediately saw in this new land other possibilities that did not include boiling pitch and cutting white pine. In droves, they abandoned Patroon Livingston's holdings, and pushed their way into what the colony's original and the real Dutch settlers named the Kaaterskill Mountains. These escapees, outlaws really, first illegally occupied an area on the eastern slope of the mountains that was part of the Hindenburg Patent. Later when these farms proved too small and unproductive and/or families grew to a size beyond what the farm could support, they abandoned them to the next wave of pioneers and pushed their version of civilization over the crest onto the western slope.

A tight knit and especially stubborn group who would pass this trait on to later generations, most of these pioneers showed their dislike for their British neighbors by opposing the King and siding with the Americans during the Revolutionary War. Once the War was over, however, and in an attempt to escape the new American government, they moved further west, settling in isolated hollows and cloves of the area that would become Palatine County. These settlers and their succeeding generations tended to be self-sufficient loners, even to the point of speaking a version of "New York Dutch" among themselves well past the point where it was no longer linguistically practical. Furthermore, they were not much into cross-cultural hybridization until the 1850's which, given the limited population, resulted in much inbreeding among those first families. While several surnames dominated—Snyder, Hover, Lawyer, Lasher, and many names beginning with "Van"—there gradually was, post1870's, an influx of newer surnames, some ending in vowels, as new immigrants discovered the area. The close-knit attitude passed down from generation to generation making the citizens of the county very leery of any kind of newcomer until the families lived among them for several generations. Only as these new bloods married into the original families where they gradually assimilated and, even then they had to adopt the attitudes, independence and lifestyles of the original settlers. Without this trait, they were ostracized and mistrusted.

Interestingly enough, Ebenezer Snyder, for whom the principal town and county seat of Palatine County was named, was actually a newcomer and not a refugee Palatine despite his surname. Rather he was fleeing a series of bad investments in New York City by moving his family west in a used covered wagon with intentions of settling in Wisconsin. However, after his wagon broke down for the fifth time and because he was tired of his wife nagging him about his lack of ability as a driver and mechanic, he said "The Hell with it," and settled on a fairly flat piece of valley land in the center of what would become the county. Subsequently, he and his wife had ten children, half of whom were girls who married well. Due to strong family ties, a small community and trading center grew up around this farm, situated as it was on the only decent north/south route through the area. Gradually this community expanded into a town, known as Snyder's Corners— complete with the apostrophe—and, finally, grew into what passed in this area as a city. The original Snyder homestead disappeared long ago although parts of the courthouse and county office building were on what the local historian believed, appropriately enough, to have been Ebenezer's barnyard. Aside from lending his name to the county's only city, Ebenezer also added an entrepreneurial spirit to the genes of some of the county's residents.

The original settlers of the area were primarily subsistence farmers with no interest in anything but procreation. The addition of these entrepreneurs, who gave little consideration to the local ecology, transformed the county. The hills, once covered with huge hemlock trees, were, by 1900, denuded so the bark could be used for tanning leather. With the trees gone, the hills eroded and the silt washed down to choke the streams making them alternately conduits for floodwater and dry streambeds. Many of the fish and wildlife that occupied the area disappeared. With the soil gone, most of the farmsteads produced less, and except for those in the broader stream valleys where farmers had the advantage of hills for pasture and valleys for crops, these marginal areas could no longer support families. Consequently they either left or went into other lines of work.

By the time the Great Depression delivered a deathblow to these small farms, most of which had already been abandoned, the population of the area was sparser still. What few people remained allowed their land to go back to forest, as their children moved from the area to seek jobs elsewhere. The salvation, at least for the moment, appeared with the election of FDR and implementation of his New Deal. The first of the WPA projects in the area was the building of a state-of-the art post office in Snyder's Corners. The second project was even more important to the economics of the county: the construction of a major, state highway along the north to south corridor through the county. This highway—number 618 in the New York State DOT system—linked the Mohawk Valley and Capital District to the north with Pennsylvania and, ultimately, New York City to the south. This allowed goods to move rapidly through the area and made it possible for the Civil Conservation Corps to be brought in.

With all the abandoned land, most of it owing state and local taxes to the point where the local governments had foreclosed on it, the state had acres of vacant land that needed to be improved. This improvement meant reforestation. To achieve this the CCC planted hundreds of thousands of seedling Scotch pine, balsam fir, and Norway spruce trees, row upon row, for acre after acre on this state land. The young men of the CCC, under the tutelage of army drill sergeants who made sure the rows were as straight as the men who planted them, worked every summer to make the area a better place. Moreover, it worked.

After time, this combination of abandoned farmland, which provided cover and forage and the stabilizing effect of the newly planted trees, which held back the soil and water, the streams came back and the wildlife returned. Helped by a massive stocking program, the county's stream and lakes soon recovered, not necessarily with native fishes but at least with stocked, nonnative species that anglers wanted to catch. The forest became a hunter's paradise at a time when many were beginning to want to reconnect with their rural past and go afield to kill something for the table. Wild turkeys reappeared as did the native black bear and it was not long before the number of whitetail deer in the county was triple that of the human population.

The influx of federal and state money put something in most of the population's pockets and gave a brief feeling of prosperity to the county—although they did not turn their backs on their Republican Party roots. Not only was the tourist trade a boon to the economy but federal funds provided for the laying of railroad track along the edge of Route 618. This rail service allowed freight, primary forest products and quarry stone, to move out of the county. This created a brief uptick in the economy that allowed the city of Snyder's Corners to grow and prosper during the latter part of the 1940's and into the early 1950's. Once this boom was over, however, the economy sunk back into a morass whereby some residents were forced into some unsavory and tax-free activities, many (such as methamphetamines, marijuana growing, drug dealing and prostitution) were clearly against the law. Fortunately for these perpetrators, the county was too poor to afford to discourage these violations.

This poverty was because the county lacked a decent tax base. Throughout their history, the local voters had stubbornly resisted breaking up the county or allowing its annexation by neighboring counties—who really did not want it either. With the tanneries long gone and the prime trees a memory, the county's revenue stream was dependant on only a few industries of any consequence: bluestone quarrying, some lumbering—primarily pulpwood production—and a few small manufacturing jobs that, as labor cost increased, would be shipped overseas. With the loss of these businesses plus the Federal aid to the railroad drying up, the railroad line shut down and, with it, the ability to bring in more industries. Aside from a few, shrinking in number, dairy farms and seasonal tourist trade, the county government and school boards were being squeezed between caring for a growing population and a shrinking tax base.

Therefore, Palatine County's lack of wealth showed. The county law enforcement was the sole providence of an elected, Republican sheriff and consisted of twenty deputies half of whom were part-timers, all of whom had no more than a year or two of experience. To hold down costs, there was no county jail—anyone needing incarnation was farmed out to nearby counties—and the county courts convened in Snyder's Corners only once a year. This meant the elected, Republican, district attorney's job was, essentially part-time and he was paid accordingly.

The highway department, which was the second largest county employer after social services, consisted of seasonal employees—most of whom were related to or knew a county legislator—whose main jobs were to sand and plow roads in the winter. What summer work needed to be done was limited to a rotating schedule of pothole filling and an occasional bridge replacement or road resurfacing if state and/or federal funds were available. Generally too, contractors from out of the county performed this kind of work—often getting the job meant providing a service or kickback to someone on the Board of Supervisors. Since the majority of the secondary roads in the county were unpaved and gravel, they required little year-round maintenance at any rate and a simple road grader running over them sometime during the early summer was sufficient. Since most of this work was seasonal, the employees filed for welfare on the off-season.

Additionally, while there was a county run landfill, there was no county-wide trash collection agency. Rather, each individual land/ home owner was responsible for arranging collection through private haulers. Since this created added home owning expenses, most simply opted to take care of their refuse by the easiest means possible. While, for some, this meant hauling their garbage to the landfill and paying a fee, many residents just simply burned most of what they could and dumped the nonflammable stuff in the nearest ravine. This caused some concern to the county's greener population since it polluted the air and water—much of which would eventually end up in New York City reservoirs. These protests on occasion even reached the ears of the county's officials. They would debate the problem, pass a few more restrictions on burning and solve the rest of it by raising fees at the landfill. Since this only added to the cost of using this facility without solving any problem, it only served to increase the illegal burning/ dumping and put the burden on the towns in the county to stop it.

Aside from Snyder's Corners, where the sheriff's department was headquartered, there was really no way for these towns to enforce any laws. These outlying towns were just loose collections of buildings including a town meeting hall, a highway department garage to house a snowplow, a shuttered general store and a gas station. Only two, Ferrioville and Henderson, had their own volunteer fire departments and post offices—the rest of the mail being rural delivery from either these facilities or Snyder's Corners. Town elections were usually over as soon as the Republicans caucused and rarely did most of the population vote on off-year elections. It was rare, too that the local Democratic Party ran anyone in opposition since it was pointless: most of the locals could not have found that line on the ballot even if someone were to have outlined it in luminous ink. Once every twenty years or so, a Democrat actually ran and won an election for a local office—even rarer was this a county-wide office and then only if there was some local issue that really turned the voters against the Republican candidate. Usually, too, the Democrat lost the office at the end of their first term.

As a result, being well affiliated with the Republican Party was a necessity if anyone wanted to get any kind of job done. This gave the party's leadership a great deal of power both in and out of the county's government. If one were to somehow run afoul of the head of the Republican Party they could find life in the county very difficult since the party controlled not only the purse strings but the only law enforcement body in the county. Without this protection, one would be better off leaving the area. On the other hand, if one were in the good graces of the party they could expect to be rewarded in any number of ways, including having law enforcement look the other way at most of their infractions.

This did not mean the citizens, in general, were lawless or Republicans. It just meant that there were elements of the population that fit this mold which were increasing in numbers due to attrition. Since the best and ablest of Palatine's youth were leaving as soon as they graduated from the county's single high school this left only those with no ambition or education as an ever increasing majority. On the other hand, the county was actually increasing in population. This increase was due to an influx of newcomers drawn to the area because the county's cost of living was considerably lower than that of downstate. As a result, people were simply selling their downstate homes and moving into the area. For a few thousand dollars, a large enough plot of land could be purchased to either hold a doublewide trailer or, if more money was available, a modular home. Often the difference between the selling price of their downstate home and the building of their new one in Palatine county was such that the newcomer was able to get by for a year or two with only a marginal job. Unlike earlier influxes of newcomers, none of these new residents were interested in improving the county. Once the money ran out, they just went on welfare.

Consequently, over half of Palatine County's budget went for social services, either administrating or paying welfare and Medicaid. The remainder of the budget was split between the highway department, law enforcement and the county's administrative costs—the latter including expenses for the board of supervisors who paid themselves more than enough to make the inconvenience of serving on the board worthwhile. The biggest job for this Board, with its one hundred percent Republican membership, was to deal with this financial crisis brought on by a loss of revenue.

As the economy changed, so did Snyder's Corners. Once the shopping hub of the county with many stores catering to a diverse and relatively well-off population, the business district was now reduced to those few stores that filled immediate needs of the welfare based population or the occasional tourist. As such, they included a drug store, liquor store, funeral home, small medical clinic, the post office, the local bank, pizza parlor, two small dinettes that were open only for breakfast and lunch, the local tavern, a couple of bed and breakfasts, and two antique "shoppes". The latter two facilities were open only from May until October for tourist season. There was no longer a grocery store but this need was filled by a convenience store, the Stop 'N Go out at the northern edge of town on Route 618 which sold gas, groceries, and NYS lottery tickets. Across the street from the store was Maggie's Diner and Truck Stop where both the truckers and their rigs could get lubed—the truck stop being a hangout for female, trucker groupies or "sisters of the road" as it where. The majority of buildings in what had been downtown Snyder's Corners was now low income— read welfare—apartments.

While most blamed the economy for the demise of the businesses in the city, there was another, bigger reason: the automobile. With Oneonta close by with its mall, Wal-Mart Super store, B-J's and other nationally advertised stores, it was easy to hop in the car and do one's shopping there. Even the increase in gas prices was offset by the lower prices so, except for those with limited mobility, few spent their money in Snyder's Corners or Palatine County. Of course, this meant that even the money from the welfare checks, once the recipients cashed them at the local bank, went out of the county. This further eroded the ability of any local merchants to compete with the stores in Otsego County.

Given the above, it was not surprising that there was little interest in the simpler, more expensive hobbies such as golf, tennis, stamp collecting, orchids, tropical fish, model airplanes and electric trains.

Other than TV watching (Fox News being the main attraction), snowmobile and ATV races along with hunting and fishing, the biggest pastime for the majority of the male population consisted of heavy drinking.

This does not mean there was no one with money in Palatine County and Snyder's Corners. In fact, considering the populations of the two places, there were more millionaires per capita in Palatine County than New York County. These included people like the quarry and pulp mill owners, heirs of the founders of the local bank, a few farmers who had sold large holdings for development (including an Indian casino in the northern corner of the county) and many who made their money elsewhere, invested well, and retired to the area to take advantage of the low taxes and low cost of living. There would be more as soon as the natural gas drilling problems were resolved and those companies interested in drilling into the Marcellus Shale could overcome the objections of downstaters worried about their water supply. Most of these lived in a single, exclusive area of the city or outside of the city at the end of long, paved driveways, marked well to prevent trespassing, on the hills overlooking some of the prettiest scenery in the eastern United States. These people were often absent for about six months of the year, escaping the county's worst weather by wintering in warmer areas of the eastern hemisphere from Miami to Antigua.

Most of the wealthier citizens were known to the locals only as the "country club crowd" as they belonged to the Kaaterskill Country Club located just north of town. The club, which had tennis courts, an Olympic-sized swimming pool, an eighteen-hole golf course and huge clubhouse was the exclusive home to this moneyed group. While there were a few young members, the average age of the males exceeded seventy, while the women's age averaged about ten to fifteen years younger due to the fact many of the men were on their second, trophy-wife marriages. At any rate, this group controlled the politics and, as a result, the finances of the county. That they cared little for or were out of touch with, the rest of the population was not important, it was just how things were. In addition, within this group there was a frostiness between those who made their money in the county and the retired downstaters who were tolerated but not especially trusted. They did have one thing in common, their political party affiliation; excepting for a few eccentrics, both groups were rock-ribbed Republicans. This party membership pretty much allowed them to do as they pleased as long as they were discrete about it.

This mistrust gave rise to strange contests between old and new families, be it on the golf course, tennis courts, business or personal ventures. The rivals walked a narrow line between "winning" whatever they were competing in and not alienating their opponents to the point where they would lose the monetary support necessary to hold their political positions. Some of these competitions included seeing who would die with the most toys. Within six months one of their members, a toy train hobbyist, would take this latter requirement literally.

— Prologue —

RICHARD NELSON HAD PUT in a long day and was tired. He had spent most of his shift doing the finishing soldering on reversing units for the final ten O-gauge versions of a special run of New York Central Hudsons. His was the very last step in the production of each model and he had just assembled and placed the fiftieth (and last) unit on the test track in front of him. Assured that it was operating correctly, he removed it and after attaching the locomotive and tender to a heavy cardboard carrier, slid both into the white, orange and blue box, which was Lionel's trademark. Satisfied that the unit had been inserted correctly so there was a good view of the locomotive and tender through an opening in the side of the box, Richard sealed the box with a piece of tape and placed it in a heavy, previously addressed, cardboard shipping carton. Sealing the end of the carton with mailing tape, he placed it in the pile with the other forty-nine boxes.

"*Ah,*" he thought. "*Finally, the last one.*"

He was the only worker left on the factory floor and was still at work because there was a deadline on this model's production. Reaching for the switch and shutting off the test track, he closed down the operation of his table for the night. Looking out through the windows of the factory, he could see a late, heavy, wet, April snow was falling on the streets of Irvington, New Jersey. It was going to be a cold, wet walk home.

Nelson was one of half a dozen highly skilled craftsmen working on a special project that was the brainchild of Josh Cowen, the owner of the Lionel Corporation based in Irvington. Richard and this select group were hand-constructing fifty O-gauge models of the Hudson for a chosen group of Lionel's dealers as a token of Lionel's (and Cowan's) appreciation. The locomotive and its tender represented a first for Lionel, an experiment into 1:48 scale and die cast construction with as much detail as the current state of the art would allow for a three-rail model. The whole of this project was a unique one for Lionel and was not like any train set they had ever produced or would again for a number of years. Also, for the first time, the engine and its tender were to receive a specific railroad line name—previously Lionel simply used the Lionel name for their locomotives. It would be a prototype of a New York Central Hudson and so labeled.

Each replica was fitted with the latest in Lionel's innovations—many of which had come to Lionel from other manufacturers that were bankrupted and then brought up by Cowen—which meant a realistic steam whistle and a reversing unit that changed direction with each interruption of power to the track. The addition of this latter unit was Richard's specialty—that and being sure everything ran correctly before it was boxed for shipment—and, since this was the final step on this last unit, it meant the project was completed for shipment to dealers in time for Christmas, 1929 sale. It also meant Richard had completed his quota for the month and would have a bonus in time for his family's brief vacation to the Jersey shore in July.

The finished models were now ready for shipment within the next day or so to a select group of Lionel dealers in and around the New York City area with a few going as far west as Chicago and Madison, Wisconsin. They were a reward to each of these dealers for doing an especially good job of moving Lionel merchandise over the last few years. Since extra care had gone into their production, these models were different from anything currently on the market and it meant the dealer had the option of keeping them as mementos, selling them at a premium or using them for gifts. Richard had learned the suggested selling price of each model was going to be over two hundred-fifty dollars: more than he had made in salary since the first of the year. He could not help but wonder at who would pay that much money for what was, essentially, a toy, but it was not his problem. With that thought, he pulled his cloth coat tightly around his body to keep as much of the damp out as possible, shut off the lights and went home.

The last thing Richard noticed was the name on the fiftieth box. It was addressed to Palatine Hardware, 23 Main Street, Snyder's Corners, New York, Attn.: William Lawyer. Richard could not help but wonder: *Where in Hell is Snyder's Corners?*

— Chapter 1 —

THERE WAS A HUGE wad of paper stuck to the face of the clock above and behind Bill Weaver's head. How and when it got there, he had no idea, but apparently one of his third period social studies students had fired it from someplace in the room. He chose to ignore it for the time being and just hoped he would remember to get rid of it before the end of the day so the custodians would not know how undisciplined some of his classes were. Although they could probably figure it out from other clues left around the room, like the "Fuck Weaver" gouged into the top of one of the desks.

It was a Tuesday, which, after Mondays, was the worst day of the teaching week. The students had recovered from the weekend and it was just far enough from Friday to discourage them from making weekend plans. Therefore, they took their frustration out on the teachers and their fellow students in the form of inattentiveness and harassment. Unfortunately, too, since it was only the third week of October, it was early in the school semester so that even the threat of final exams was not a deterrent.

Bill was getting sick of the whole thing. Having taught eighth grade students in the Rye Junior/Senior High School for twenty-nine years, he had seen it all and was reaching the end of his tether. He remembered that during his first few years some of the more experienced teachers had lamented about how student behavior was deteriorating badly as the years went on. Bill had laughed and just dismissed those complaints as the onset of old age. Now that he found himself in the latter stages of his career, he could not help but agree. Kids today were worse than their parents had been.

Was he coming down with burnout? He was not sure, but between increased New York State Education Department regulations, parental pressure, asinine requests from the administration, more testing, and increased discipline problems, Bill found himself looking more and more toward retirement. Fortunately, he was Tier One in the New York State Teachers' Retirement system so he could go out anytime after fifty-five. He found himself already counting down the days of those five remaining years.

Thank God and the teachers' union for a free period, he thought. At least he could get out of his room and get a shot of coffee. Slowly, Bill pushed himself up from his desk and grabbed the folder of essays on the causes of the Civil War that his honors class had turned in that morning. He knew that half would be direct, word for word, copies from the Internet while the rest would be a jumble of misspellings and grammatical mistakes. Either way, they were something he had to wade through since if the students realized how little he cared about what they had written, they might revolt. This kind of assignment was one of the many requirements handed down by the powers above to get the students to do more writing, with emphasis on quantity not quality. As with most of these added requirements, it was done without regard to the amount of extra work it made for those teachers who felt they actually had to correct this stuff.

Bill poked his head out the classroom door and checked for stragglers in the hall. Since classes had already passed and the halls were clear, the trip to the faculty room would be uneventful, without the usual jostling and banter from the students. So, aside from making his obligatory stop at the boy's restroom, his duties were over for one, fifty-minute period.

After checking each stall for smokers, Bill could not help but catch sight of himself in the mirror. He noted that, for a guy just at fifty, he still did not appear to have aged that much. His hair was still light blond and, if he sucked it in, his paunch was not especially noticeable. While in high school he had been a fairly decent athlete. At an even six feet and one hundred-eighty pounds, he had been a fairly good tight end and defensive back in football and sixth man on the Rhinebeck High School basketball varsity his senior year. He was good enough to consider walking on the football team in college but opted for the social life rather than put up with the training. Still, he played pickup basketball with the faculty team up until he turned forty at which point he realized he was taking more time to recover from the exertion than he wanted to. So now he confined his team sports to slow-pitch softball in a beer league during the summer months where he caught and batted cleanup. Aside from that, he played a number of rounds of golf during the warmer months of the year. While he was good enough to carry a 9 handicap, he limited his actual physical activity to getting in and out of a golf cart for most his rounds.

Other than those pursuits, his main exercise came as part of his vocation. He was the type of teacher who while in the classroom, kept moving, constantly observing his students and not making himself a stationary target. It occurred to him that all this moving around probably kept him in shape and looking younger. Ruminating on this, he pushed his way out of the bathroom door and made the rest of the trip to the teachers' lounge.

Once inside the room, Bill gave a general greeting to the few teachers who were sitting around the main table, tossed the folder down in front of one of the empty chairs, took his coffee cup down from the rack and filled it. He tossed a quarter in the jar next to the coffee urn to pay for what passed as coffee, stirred in some sugar and cream using a communal spoon, and set the filled cup down next to his place at the table.

"More papers to correct, I see." Mildred Kline looked up from her class book as Bill took his seat. Mildred was also a social studies teacher but in the high school. A few years younger than Bill, they had dated seriously a few years ago but mutually broke it off. Since neither one was willing to make a total commitment, they decided their relationship was not going anywhere and parted on amicable terms. Bill's biggest concerns, other than a past divorce, stemmed from the fact they were colleagues and he was struggling to make it on a teacher's salary while paying alimony and child support. While there was definitely an attraction, they just remained on a friendly basis.

"Yeah, this time it is the honors class so some will be reasonably intelligent reading. At least those copied from someplace on the Internet." Bill smiled as he flipped open the folder and took out the first essay and a red pen from his shirt pocket.

"Probably they used Wikipedia."

"What in hell is that?" Bill was puzzled by Mildred's reference.

"Oh, that's right, you're a Luddite. I forgot: no computer and no cell phone." While Mildred was needling Bill, she was also vexed by his lack of interest in these two modern appliances.

"I'm not a Luddite, exactly, I just don't trust that stuff." In truth Bill was not willing to put his faith in cyber gadgets. For one thing he was frightened by all the stories of identity theft stemming from computer use that were constantly in the news and, as a consequence, was one of the few on the faculty that had neither a computer nor a cell phone. Nor did he want either one. "Besides that, those damn cell phones can't get service where you need them anyway. I try talking to someone that is using one and they break up or get cut off. Why anyone would want one is beyond me."

"That may be true but don't you find it annoying that your students are more computer savvy than you?" Mildred was smiling.

"Not really. But when they finally get a computer that will grade these damn papers, then I might be interested in one. I suspect I'm going to be doing this by hand for a long time."

"Sure would be nice if the guys in the front office and state department who think we should be assigning more of this kind of thing were to come down and correct some of them."

"Yeah, and could, somehow, convince the kids that the writing they were doing for social studies and English classes were to be done in the same language." Bill had already circled the misspelling of the "Fart Sumpter" which he assumed was for "Fort Sumter" and underlined two partial sentences that made absolutely no sense. "It would help if the kids had some typing skills too. Hell, I'll give this one credit; at least he tried to copy from the website rather than just print it off."

"Makes you wonder if they think we won't actually read what they hand in."

"Ok, face it, a lot of teachers don't. You can't blame the kids for trying to get away with it with all their classes." Bill was beginning to worry if his red pen would have enough ink to get him through the period without returning to his room for another one.

"I agree. Laziness falls on both sides of the desk, I would guess." Mildred rose and went to the urn to refill her cup. "God, it seems like I need more and more of this stuff just to keep going." Smiling, she sat down and began copying marks from the student's papers into her class book.

Engrossed in trying to decipher a paragraph that was either about slavery or salivary—even having a spell-check program was no help to some of them—Bill did not notice the secretary from the main office enter the room until she tapped him on the shoulder.

"Mr. Weaver?" It was a question even though she knew perfectly well who he was since she not only had been a secretary in the system since graduating from high school three years ago but also was one of his former students. "You have a phone call in the office."

Had this been a normal classroom, the public address system that was wired into every room of the school would have been used to deliver this message. However, one time when the office secretary called in to inquire about a student, she left the return speaker on a little too long and the assembled faculty batted around unkind but truthful comments about the student without realizing it was being picked up and relayed back to the office. Inasmuch as the open mike transmitted these unflattering observations into the office and since the parent was standing within hearing distance of the main console, there had been fallout that placed the principal in an embarrassing position. Consequently, the PA system in the faculty room was rewired so only general announcements could be heard in the teachers' room and there was no two-way communication between the room and the office. Now, in order to get a message to a teacher, a secretary or a passing student had to be used to walk the dozen or so steps from the office to the faculty room to deliver it.

"Ok." Bill put down his pen and closed the folder. "Who from, do you know?"

"It is a woman who says she is your mother."

Bill was curious why his mother would be calling him at school but relieved that it was not a parent of one of his students.

"Hello." The phone lay on the counter in the office and Bill picked it up.

"Billy?" It was his mother's voice and she sounded as if she had been crying. His first thoughts were that something had happened to his eighty-two year old father.

"Yes, Mom, it is me. What's the matter?"

"Uncle William has died."

Uncle William? Bill had to stop and think for a moment to place his mother's brother. Of course, his uncle William Lawyer—never Bill or Will, always William—was his mother's only sibling. For years he had been the sole operator of the family's hardware/toy store in the upstate city of Snyder's Corners until the economics of the area caused him to abruptly shut down the shop in the early nineteen eighties'. Bill was in his late twenties at the time and away from home. The last time he had visited his uncle was when he was in his preteens, fifteen or so years prior to that. His most vivid memory was of spending hours poking around the store and the storage area on the floor above it. However, once he reached puberty and, having discovered girls, Bill was no longer interested in hardware or toys so had stopped making the upstate trip. In fact, he had not thought much about his uncle William in about thirty years and only vaguely knew his uncle had been in a nursing home for the last ten or so years.

"When? How?" Bill could not think of anything else to say.

"Apparently last night in his sleep. The nursing home called this morning. He was, after all, ninety-one, so it isn't a surprise, just a shock." His mother seemed a bit calmer now. "The funeral is on Friday at ten o'clock in Snyder's Corners and I hope you will be able to come."

"Of course, I have a lot of family days coming to me I can certainly take one or two for my uncle's funeral. Should I come by and pick you and Pop up or will you get up there some other way?"

"No, we'll be fine, Dear. Your father is a good driver and we can get as far as Snyder's Corners with no trouble."

Yeah, Bill thought, *Dad's a good driver. Hah!* His father was eighty-two, diabetic, with failing eyesight and almost total hearing loss, not to mention slow reflexes. Fortunately when he got behind the wheel he drove slowly and his mother did most of the navigation by shouting "Harold, look out for that!" when anything appeared to be menacing. Bill just pitied anyone who happened to be stuck behind them in traffic between Rhinebeck and Snyder's Corners.

"OK Mom, I'll meet you at the funeral home in Snyder's Corners sometime before ten on Friday. If I remember the city correctly, there can be no more than one funeral home so it shouldn't be a problem. You make sure Pop drives carefully now. Love you." Bill was about to hang up wanting to get some work done before the end of his free period.

"Oh Billy?" His mother always insisted on adding the "y" to his name, something he had dropped as soon as he graduated from high school and gone away to college.

"Yes?"

"Would you call Amy and tell her about Uncle William? I never seem to be able to get hold of her and you always manage to. Maybe she would be interested in going to the funeral too."

Amy was Bill's sister, a dozen years younger, thrice divorced and now single; she was living in New York City and working in New Jersey. Estranged from her parents for reasons never made clear to him, Bill was the only family member that managed to keep track of his wayward sister, who, despite two undergrad years at Vassar, was currently working as a waitress in a diner on Route 7 in Paramus.

"Sure, I'll give her a call. If she's interested in going, I'll swing by and pick her up. See you on Friday." Bill really had to get back to his papers.

"Thank you, Dear. By the way, the name of the funeral home is Gates and Sons and it is right on Main Street. See you on Friday. Bye." There was a click on the other end of the line.

Bill went back to the faculty room and picked up the folder. With only five minutes left in his free period, he had corrected exactly two papers, leaving him another twenty-four to go. This meant he was going to have to work late tonight not only correcting papers, but also making lesson plans for Friday so whoever substituted for him would have something to do. Luckily, since it was a Friday, he could plan to give the students a test, assuming he had time to write one up. Of course, too, it would mean more papers to correct when he got back. Dumping the half-cup of cold coffee into the sink and replacing the mug on the rack, he took his folder of papers and trudged back to his classroom. Mentally preparing himself for the rest of the day, he moved his Uncle William and Snyder's' Corners to the back of his mind.

Damn, he thought, *I should have told them in the office while I was still there. I'm gonna want Friday off.* He made a mental note to tell them on his way to lunch duty.

— Chapter 2 —

Thomas Bisignani saw William Lawyer's obituary in the Oneonta Star. Tom always checked the obits first thing upon opening the paper to see if any of his peers had passed on. He joked with is wife, Becky, that he needed to check to see if he was listed just to make sure he should make plans for the day. Not that his demise was imminent as Tom was, at seventy-four and aside from a few aches and pains, in excellent health, the result of a lifetime of working outdoors. He prided himself in being able to keep up with men half his age when it came to lifting and hauling.

Tom had several memories of William Lawyer but he especially remembered the combined hardware and toy store the Lawyer family ran in Snyder's Corners. Foremost in this recollection was Lawyer's display of electric trains in the store window every Christmas. It was always one of the highlights of Tom's early years to stand, nose pressed to the window, watching the trains make their circuit of the track, ducking under tunnels in the snow-covered mountains only to reappear in the opposite corner of the display. A preteen boy could lose himself in this action. Second, and maybe more importantly, it was from Lawyer's store that his father had purchased Tom's first electric train set. It had been in 1938 and the train set had consisted of a used Lionel, Union Pacific streamline steam locomotive with four matching passenger cars, twenty feet of track and two manually operated switches. For an eight-year old boy, it was the best Christmas present ever and, even as a used set, probably set his father, who was a logger, back a couple of week's salary.

It was worth it though for both Tom and his dad. Together, they spent hours playing with the train, first around the Christmas tree and later when they jointly built a year-round layout in the basement. It was an activity the two shared until Tom's teen years when he became interested in other pursuits. The set was then relegated to the cellar where, if his father remembered, it made an annual reappearance at Christmas.

Years later, while Tom was serving in the Marines in Korea and the spring after his father had died, his mother cleaned out the cellar so she could sell the house. Since this was years before yard sales and eBay, she discarded everything she found there, including the locomotive, cars, track and accessories he and his dad had added, plus Tom's set of baseball cards. Along with the rest of the trash, a local hauler trucked them to the county landfill. Had Tom ever gone into analysis, the psychiatrist would probably have found the trauma of this had caused a deep-seated psychosis that affected some of Tom's subsequent relationships and life-style.

At the time, however, it had little effect on Tom who, upon returning to civilian life, needed fulltime employment. Having no education beyond high school, and with his only life skills being able to take orders and shoot a rifle, he managed to find a job as a miner in a bluestone quarry outside of Snyder's Corners. It took him only a couple of weeks to realize that cutting and lifting stone in a quarry was not where he wanted to spend his working career. To this end, Tom began manipulating his fellow workers in such a way that Tom ended up with the best jobs and/or the most money for doing them. After only six months, Mr. Meyers, the quarry owner, noticed this quality in Tom and recognized a callousness in his personality which Meyers felt would be best used in selling stone. So Tom was pulled out of the quarry and put to work in the yard or, as it should more properly be called, stone dock, with the job of salesman. It was in this capacity that

Tom was sent by Mr. Meyers to help deliver a railcar load of stone to New York City.

It was on this trip where Tom found his calling. By managing to negotiate an increase of ten dollars more a ton once the load reached the City, Tom not only increased the profit on the load but impressed his boss. He did this by skillfully, and secretly, playing off two distributors against one another. When he returned, Mr. Meyers was so impressed that he put Tom in charge of distribution. After five years on the job and by carefully saving his commissions and an increasing number of under-the-table payoffs from distributors, Tom was able to buy the quarry and dock from a retiring Mr. Meyers. Ten years later by using the inside information from his earlier contact with distributors, he was able to ruthlessly manipulate prices to put the local competition at a disadvantage and out of business. Tom then brought up the bankrupt businesses. By the late 1970's Tom owned all five of the quarries in Palatine County giving him a monopoly on the sales and distribution of bluestone from the area. If a contractor wanted what was, arguably, the finest bluestone in the country, he had to pay Tom Bisignani's price.

For those not familiar with it, bluestone is a very hard sedimentary type of sandstone that is rich in quartz and colored by the iron pigment that was mixed in with the sediment. While some of the best is blue in color, it can vary from brown to pink to green depending on the how the iron in the rock oxidized. Quarried or mined in the Catskills of New York and parts of northeast Pennsylvania, it was an extremely important material of choice in the early nineteen hundreds for sidewalks in small towns and big cities up and down the coast. (Many of the sidewalks of New York City were and are bluestone that was hauled out of the Catskills and floated down the Hudson River to the City.) Later, due to improved methods of mining and techniques in cutting and polishing, it became available to anyone building up-scale homes in the northern New Jersey, eastern Pennsylvania, Westchester County or out on Long Island. Contractors first just used it in sidewalks and entries but soon found customers wanted it in their foyers, around their pools, even as kitchen floors and, eventually, as counter tops. Given its versatility and the natural beauty most who saw it in other's homes, wanted bluestone someplace in theirs as well. When the housing boom of the 1960's and 70's occurred, Tom Bisignani was in an ideal position to make a large profit in the market.

It did not take long before the Bisignani Bluestone dock was shipping train carloads and later, after the railroad stopped serving the area, semi-trailer loads of the newly quarried bluestone downstate. The market was not confined to the Greater New York City area, either. Soon dealers were shipping boatloads of Bisignani Bluestone to Miami and, via the Panama Canal, to California, even Hawaii. Tom often had his miners working under lights just to keep up with the demand.

This, of itself, was propelling Tom Bisignani on the way to becoming millionaire by the age of fifty and toward a satisfying retirement. He would have been content in this position but, as luck would have it, he added a second, even more profitable, product to his line. It happened quite by accident.

One of Tom's buyers, having made a trip up from Westchester County to visit him in Snyder's Corners, noticed the stone walls around the edge of the quarry's property. He inquired as to whether it would be possible for Tom to ship him some of that stone so he could build a similar wall around the development he was constructing. Tom said that, for a price, he would be glad to do it. After Tom and the contractor agreed on a price to make it worth his while, Tom had a couple of his miners stack a dozen pallets with the rock from one of the walls and then shipped it downstate. A week later, the contractor called and wanted more stone. Within a month, Tom was shipping a thousand pallets a week to interested contractors and the price per pallet was increasing.

The pioneer farmers of the northeastern United States from Maine down to the Carolinas had one big problem with their land. The area was covered repeatedly by glaciers which, when they melted left behind more rock than soil. In order to effectively farm this land, these rocks, some larger than a good-sized ox, others as small as a man's fist, had to be removed so a plow could be applied to and stay in the soil. Whether done by hand picking or specially designed rock pickers, this rock removal was an annual job for many of the farmers, their sons, daughters, even their wives. Loaded into oxen powered sledges, this rock had to be disposed of in some way. While they dumped a large amount of it into some handy ravine or an out of the way pile, many of these early farmers were more resourceful than that. With little knowledge of engineering but a lot of practical ability, these farmers (and their sons, daughters and wives) carefully stacked this rock into fences, foundations, and, even, buildings. Sometimes, especially in buildings, mortar was used, but, most often the rock was simply balanced, one upon the other, into walls two or three feet high. These walls fenced in fields, defined property lines and, when topped with branches or a tree trunk or two to make them higher, deterred livestock from wandering off. While they required some annual maintenance—early spring, before the plowing and planting season started was considered prime time for restacking walls that had been toppled by frost—these fences became a permanent part of the landscape, lasting far longer than the farms they surrounded and the men who built them. Property in Palatine County was outlined with thousands of miles of stone fences.

These rock walls were considered quaint. Artists painted pictures of them on abandoned land, along dirt roads and rambling through mixed stands of hardwood. Photographers used miles of film on them, usually in connection with autumn leaves or covered with snow, printing the resulting photos in books to grace coffee tables or in calendars. Robert Frost even wrote a poem about their maintenance. To the locals, however, they were just there and little or no thought was given to them. That was changed when Tom Bisignani and his like discovered there was a demand for the stone.

A local farmer, stooped from years of removing stone, once remarked that his best crop was rock, if only there was a market for it. His heirs found that market.

The method of packaging the rock was a fairly simple but labor intensive one in which the amount of money changing hands increased the higher one went in the process. First, the primary operator contracted with local farmers and landowners for their fences and rock piles. Once a suitable source was found a price per pallet was offered—generally this was five to ten dollars each, depending on the accessibility of the rock. Considering that many rock walls might contain several hundred or more pallets of rock, this was more money than most farmers would see from their milk checks in a year. Next came the rock stackers, usually men, older teenaged boys, and, in some cases, women, who went out to the walls, foundations, and piles to dig out and stack the rock on pallets. Over the years, many rock walls had sunk into or become buried by the soil from the surrounding fields so the stackers first had to dig them out of the ground. This was hard work often done in wet, raw weather and requiring the use of shovels, picks, crowbars and, occasionally, heavy machinery. By the time the three by three-foot pallets, made from locally harvested hardwood, were stacked about three feet high with rock and secured with heavy chicken wire, a considerable amount of energy had been expended. Usually the primary contractor paid the stackers by the pallet, generally five or six dollars per unit. Most good skilled stackers could fill eight to ten pallets in a dawn to dusk day, which, considering the economics of the area and the type of person who went into this line of work was good, tax-free money. Finally, the primary contractor came in with a front loader and flatbed truck, loaded up the pallets and took them to the Bisignani dock where he might receive thirty to fifty dollars a pallet on his investment of eleven to sixteen dollars.

Bisignani, who served as a broker for hundreds of these small-time, primary operators, had the Palatine County version of this market to himself—something Tom ruthlessly exploited. He earned a reputation of being a tough person to cross and one that usually got what he wanted.

Once the pallets were delivered and stacked in his yard, Bisignani had them loaded on a semi and transported to downstate dealers where the going price was one hundred fifty to two hundred dollars a pallet. Considering this profit in terms of the amount of investment involved and lack of any liability, it was no wonder Tom closed two of his bluestone quarries and sold the other four to the miners who were working them. He kept only one quarry, the original, now played out, Meyers' quarry close to town, where he had his office and receiving/transfer yard.

In this way, miles of rock walls, foundations, and rock piles disappeared from Palatine County. This caused concern for historians, county officials and law enforcement personnel. The historians feared the loss of local history—many of the foundations marked long abandoned settlements and some of the rock piles had actually marked Indian constructed encampments. The officials pointed out that most of the rock walls marked legal property boundaries as were noted on deeds and their loss would mean someone was going to have to resurvey all the boundaries. Enforcement officials had to contend with numerous cases of rock rustling. Operators and stackers sneaked onto land where they were not welcome—often trespassing on state forestland—and took rock without paying for it. Often too, since a lot of money might be involved, neighbors were pitted against neighbors as to who, exactly, owned what when it came to property line walls. Suits and countersuits broke out, much to the profit of the local lawyers.

Not that Tom minded. No longer saddled with managing his bluestone quarries his work consisted mainly of counting pallets and paying some local for them so he went into semiretirement. This freed up a lot of his time and he used this in two ways.

Early in his quarry owning career he had gotten into politics. Not that he actually ran for office. That would be too much of a demand on his time and might lead to interest in his personal life and business practices. Rather, he used his contributions to the local Republican Party to leverage his way into the local party's chairmanship. Considering that the Republican Party was the only one of consequence in the county, he became their power broker, in effect controlling the politics of Palatine County. With this power came prestige, making Tom one of the most respected people in the county. It also had certain advantages for someone in Tom's business since, from time to time, his mining operations ran afoul of the Department of Environmental Conservation—runoff in particular could pollute streams—which required some political help to resolve. In one instance when his quarry just north of Snyder's Corners began filling with ground water that threatened to flood and shut down the operation, Tom had no problem getting the necessary permits to pump this water into the creek that went through town. This was despite the fact that the water polluted the stream so badly that there was a massive die-off of fish. Later, when Tom shut down that particular quarry because it was no longer profitable, he generously offered to restock the stream which created a huge tax break for his business.

The second thing that occupied his time—obsessed it was a better word—was his collection of Lionel electric trains.

This happened quite by accident. While on a rock selling trip to Boston, Tom found himself on Cross Street in Malden, Massachusetts. Looking up, he discovered he was standing in front of a place he had never heard about nor knew existed: Charles Ro Supply Company. In the window was a display of the newest line of Lionel trains. Intrigued, Tom went inside and reverted to the eight-year old he had been in 1938 but with more money to spend. By the time he walked out, his credit card had taken over a two thousand-dollar hit and he had arranged to ship several trains, a transformer, accessories and track to his home in Snyder's Corners. Tom Bisignani had become an electric train enthusiast, big time.

Because he was an early user of computers to keep track of his stock and sales, Tom was very astute when it came to using them and had become a bit of an Internet junkie. Therefore, it was not long before Tom was buying additional locomotives, rolling stock and accessories from Internet suppliers and through eBay auctions. Tom developed a reputation for being an astute bidder on eBay but not one a seller wanted to cross by misrepresenting an item. Several shady sellers felt his ire which resulted in eBay shutting down their sites. In keeping with his childhood memories, he kept true to the Lionel brand, ignoring most of the other half dozen manufactures in the marketplace.

In particular there was an upstart company called Mike's Train House or MTH, a company started by Mike Wolf, a former Lionel employee, in direct competition to Lionel. As time went on, Tom and others of his ilk became convinced that MTH was a symbol of what was wrong, specifically, with the electric train hobby and America in general. However, that was a prejudice that Tom would have to develop. In the beginning, he was only interested in recapturing the joys of his youth.

So it was that after Tom saw William Lawyer's obit in the Star, he journeyed not so much back into time as down into his basement where, stretching from wall to wall was his thirty-five by forty-foot, custom-built train layout. In addition to the working layout, all along three of the four walls, all in special humidity controlled cabinets was a collection of vintage Lionel locomotives and accessories. Although this collection would be irreplaceable (the insured value was for two million dollars), it represented one of the larger, if not largest, private collections of its type in the country. Tom Bisignani had been a busy man.

Like most collectors, Tom had made no plan as to what was to become of this collection once he passed on. Tom and his first wife, Ramona, had no children. After she died of ovarian cancer in her early thirties, Tom had remained a widower until he turned sixty-eight, at which time he met Rebecca Elgin, who was thirty-five years his junior, and remarried. Additionally, after Ramona died and because he was seeking companionship, Tom had taken what he considered a necessary step to preserve his property from illegitimate heirs by having a vasectomy, therefore no children were going to come from this second union either. At those moments when he actually thought about his estate in general and collection in particular, he just figured that Becky would sell everything off at a fraction of what it was worth and enjoy spending the money. This could have made him sad except that he realized he was not going to be around for the event and it was nothing he especially needed to worry about.

He also considered, briefly, attending Lawyer's funeral not just because of the trains but because Lawyer, as a Republican Party member, had worked with Tom back thirty or so years ago. Then Tom noted that the service was to be this Friday. Since this was the third Friday in October, it was the weekend of the semi-annual York Train Meet, and there was no way Tom would miss that. At this point in his life, trains and York were more important to Tom than any long forgotten dealings he had with a minor party member. Besides, he and Jerry VanVierden always drove down together and he did want to miss the chance to argue trains with Jerry for the four-hour trip down and back.

— Chapter 3 —

WHILE TURNING THE MORNING newspaper's pages between the daily crossword puzzle and the financial page, Jeremiah (Jerry to his friends) VanVierden also saw William Lawyer's obituary in the Star. Since there was no reason for him to know the man, he simply ignored it.

Anyone noticing Jerry's last name and knowing anything about the history of Palatine County would have assumed that he was a native, but, other than having an ancestor who may have been a Palatine immigrant in his family tree, he was an outsider. He had been born and raised in northern New Jersey, graduated from Rensselaer Polytechnic Institute with a degree in civil engineering in 1956. Upon graduation he married Katrina, a coed from Russell Sage, and went to work in the New York City area primarily with architects and contractors who were building gated developments and large estate homes in NYC's suburbs.

Not only did Jerry make good money from this job, which involved laying out streets, service lines and assorted amenities that made these projects small communities unto themselves, he also was party to inside information as to the locations of future developments. This allowed him to be able to make some shrewd, timely and profitable real estate investments. Additionally, he befriended many of the people who were buying these houses. Since most were well connected to Wall Street,

18

they were able to give Jerry tips that allowed him to invest well in the market. In short, when Jerry was ready to retire, he and his wife were financially very well off. This was especially satisfying to Jerry, considering his father had only been an engineer on the Pennsylvania Railroad and a poorly paid one at that.

As the time Jerry and Katrina chose for retirement neared, they realized they did not want to remain in the NYC area. Both their sons had graduated from prestigious Ivy League schools and gone into very lucrative careers that took them far from Manhattan and Westchester County. It was for this reason that the VanVierdens began searching for a good place in upstate New York to build a retirement home. While on an antiquing trip down NYS Route 618 they happened onto Snyder's Corners. After shopping at the two stores in town, they noticed a nationally advertised realtor's for sale sign on a tract of land south of town just off the state highway. The twenty acre lot included a west-facing hillside with gorgeous vista that just cried for a home. After Jerry contacted the local representative of the real estate agency and haggled down the price so it was affordable, he contracted with one of the builders he had worked with in White Plains to put up a two story, five thousand square-foot home on the land. While it was considerably larger than either he or Katrina would ever need, it allowed Jerry to fulfill one of his lifetime hobbies.

Built at the top of the hill so that the upper story was above grade and with massive windows on the downhill side, this top floor would serve as their main living quarters. The lower level was built into the hillside using laminated beams and no supporting posts thus creating one very large room. This room was to be the home of Jerry's ultimate dream, a massive electric train layout that would accommodate his growing collection of three-rail, O-gauge, Pennsylvania Railroad locomotives, rolling stock and assorted accessories.

Jerry had originally been into the small, 1:87 scale, HO-gauge electric trains while his sons were preteenagers in part to share something with his boys and part as an outgrowth of his job. This scale allowed him to build realistic models in a small area, which satisfied his desire for precision and detail. In addition, these small models could be controlled by an automated system that allowed the trains to move around the layout without one having to hover constantly over a transformer. The fact that this system was radio operated also appealed to Jerry's engineering side. While his sons soon tired of the tiny trains that operated at scale, but exceedingly slow, speeds, Jerry became completely enamored with them and spent much of his spare time working on his model empire. He even joined a local club whose members were dedicated to building an exact replica of Pennsylvania station, surrounding Manhattan, and the NYC train yards, all in HO scale.

Then his eyesight began to change.

As Jerry approached his sixties, he began to notice that he could no longer satisfactorily manipulate the small scale locomotives and cars. Also, while he had did not seem to notice any loss of dexterity, he was also having a problem creating scenery because it seemed as though previously constructed parts kept getting in the way of his fingers. He finally concluded that he no longer had the physical capabilities to keep up with this hobby and one day announced at the HO club meeting that his whole layout was for sale. Within twenty-four hours, his entire HO layout, representing twenty-five years of work, was gone.

To a lesser man, that would have been the end of his involvement in model railroading hobby, and he would have gone into something else. In Jerry's case, whether it was his railroading background, or simple stupidity, interest in electric trains did not stop with the sale of his layout. The next day he took the twenty-five hundred dollars he had received for his layout and went out a bought his first O-gauge locomotive. It was a brand new, Mike's Train House, Pennsylvania 4-4-6-4 Q2 steam engine with a Proto-Sounds 2.0 ® operating/sound system and a set of Pennsylvania streamlined passenger cars. He also purchased a MTH Z-4000 transformer, a complete Z-4000 remote control system and about two hundred feet of track. Although the whole set cost considerably more than what he realized on the HO sale—the locomotive alone was over thirteen hundred dollars—he was completely satisfied. That night he cleared room in his basement, set up some plywood on sawhorses and built his first O-gauge lay out.

Jerry immediately liked this new gauge. At 1:48 it was twice as large as the HO (HO actually meant half O even though it is a bit bigger than that) with locomotives and rolling stock that were easier to manipulate, couple up cars, get on and off the track and, if repairs needed to be made, take apart and put back together. He could do all of this, too, without resorting to a jeweler's loupe. Additionally, the larger size allowed for more detail on both the locomotives and stock, something that had been gradually improved over the last few years to the point where the models were becoming exact, scale replicas of the real thing. This amount of detail especially appealed to Jerry, who, as his involvement increased, began to research the prototypes for the various locos and become more sophisticated in his selection of those items that were closest to the real thing. Finally, unlike the HO models, the O-gauge locomotives produced smoke and had real sounds with not only realistic whistles and bells but braking, turning and even train announcements coming from the loco or its tender. Even the chuff rate (the chugging sounds a locomotive makes as it starts and slows) matched the movement of the rods and pistons on the wheels and the puffs of smoke coming out of the stack. In short, these trains were 1:48 replicas of the real thing and Jerry was in complete love with them.

Unfortunately, these trains needed room to operate. While the track radius could be as tight as a twenty-seven-inch diameter circle, the bigger locomotives needed not only seventy-two inch radius curves or bigger to operate but to look the most realistic. Jerry's basement could not accommodate that kind of a layout. So he made do with what he had, winding track around the furnace and house support posts, taking up and tearing down each layout as he purchased more trains that needed more space. Some, in fact, could not be satisfactorily operated on any of his layouts so were relegated to shelves built around the room.

Fortunately, Jerry specialized early. Instead of buying every kind of locomotive that he saw, he stuck exclusively to the railroad of his father, specializing in Pennsylvania Rail Road steam engines. Unfortunately, there were a lot of them available for this railroad line and more coming on the market all the time. To try to control his collection to some extent, Jerry further bought only those locomotives introduced by

Mike's Train House and emphasizing the steam locomotive era. There was another reason for this loyalty. MTH was about to introduce a new operating system for their trains. It would be an entirely new digitalized system designed to give commands to not only their locomotives but also to their operating accessories. This system, unlike others on the market including that used in HO, would be computer upgradeable and compatible with other systems on the market. It promised to be revolutionary and sounded like something the civil engineer in Jerry would really enjoy.

When it finally came onto the market in 2000 and, since this coincided with the building of his new house, Jerry went for it in a big way. He even sold all of his powered units that could not be controlled or upgraded for control by this system. The system, called by MTH Digital Command System or DCS©, was unique in the O-gauge hobby in that it relied on a digitally transmitted signal going directly to the locomotive or the tender and regulated by using a remote, handheld device. While Lionel had a similar system, called TrainMaster Command Control or TMCC©, which they introduced in the nineteen nineties, theirs was not digital. Jerry was convinced that MTH's system, which would be computer upgradeable via the Internet and had more features, was the wave of the future. Besides, the DCS was compatible with TMCC—not that Jerry had any Lionel locomotives—while the reverse was not true.

Either system had a distinct advantage in the eyes of some new, electrical gadget owning, computer literate members of the train hobby, over the old-fashioned conventional method of operation. With conventional operation of electric trains which went back to the early days of Lionel, the operator controlled his single train by increasing or decreasing the amount of electricity available to the locomotive by mechanically moving handles on the transformer. Bells and whistles operate by disrupting the power with a button. With DCS or TMCC, the transformer is set at a certain voltage—usually 18 to 22 volts depending on the size of the layout and number of items to be controlled—and operation is begun by addressing a specific locomotive from the remote control device. A push of the start button on the remote brings the addressed locomotive to life. It is then put into motion by rotating a thumb wheel (DCS) or knob (TMCC) on a handheld device similar to a TV remote. The operator then can initiate whistles, bells, starts/stops, smoke, chuff rate and numerous other tasks with a push of a button that sends a signal from the handheld through a control box to the locomotive. Since each locomotive has its own address in the handheld, it is possible to operate multiple trains separately or together on a single loop or multiple loops of track in combination with one another. By the time MTH finally brought their system onto the market, Jerry was in the process of building the layout in his new home, so he was able to wire it for maximum operation with this system. The resulting layout, while in a constant state of construction, was a thing to behold.

Since money was not a problem, the layout included all the latest trackage and buildings available. In addition, a closed circuit television system with camera mounted in a locomotive allowed Jerry to operate this trains from the comfort of his upstairs den. This last item was more for guests than Jerry, since he spent most the eight months he was in residence at Snyder's Corners—he and Katrina wintered in San Juan—working on the layout or just running his trains. While Katrina enjoyed golf and just hanging out at the Kaaterskill Country Club, Jerry's sole hobby was his trains.

Considering that most of Jerry's physical exercise since his retirement involved crawling around under his layout doing wiring, he was in surprisingly good shape. He was one of those people with such a high rate of metabolism that he could eat anything he wanted and did not put on weight so stayed relatively slim His yearly physicals turned up no heart related problems, which he contributed to his complete immersion in his train hobby. In fact, he had only one health problem, but it was one that had turned into an obsession: his prostate.

During the last years on the job, he noticed he was having trouble emptying his bladder. Gradually he became more and more anxious about it so he went to a urologist for a checkup. It turned out his problem was a prostate gland that was enlarging and gradually squeezing his urethra, slowing the flow of urine. This enlargement was also causing his PSA numbers to climb which necessitated a biopsy. This invasive test, to both Jerry and Katrina's relief, turned up no sign of cancer. To relax the prostate and make it easier for him to empty his bladder, his doctor put Jerry on Flomax and told him things would be fine.

It did not turn out that way.

It might have been caused by the decongestant that he took for a stuffy nose, but one evening, shortly after he had moved to Snyder's Corners, he noticed he was having trouble peeing. At first, it did not bother him, but gradually his bladder filled and he was having more and more of a problem getting relief. The longer it went on, the more he strained and the less urine came out. Finally, after about three hours, not only was there not even a dribble, but the pressure of a filling bladder was causing excruciating pain. What Jerry had, he was to learn later, was an extreme case of Benign Prostatic Hyperplasia or BPH resulting in Acute Urine Retention (AUR). After a number of unsuccessful attempts at relief, Jerry woke his wife and asked her to get him to Oneonta to the hospital emergency room.

By the time they arrived in the ER Jerry could not walk without pain and no matter how he positioned himself he could get no relief. Fortunately, this was not the first time the attending nurse had seen this problem and she immediately set about prepping Jerry for a catheter. Inserting it was not easy. Only the pain and need for relief enabled Jerry to put up with the additional pain of having a female nurse fondle his dick in her attempt to insert a 4.7mm diameter tube into a 4 mm opening. Finally, once the nurse forced the catheter's tip through the swollen prostate and urine began to flow into the bag attached to it, was Jerry able to relax. The memory of the pain, however, was never going to leave him.

After his urologist removed the catheter and bag two weeks later, Jerry vowed that this would not happen again. As a result, care of his prostate became a passion with him. He increased the dosage of the alpha-blocker, took nettles, saw palmetto and pygeum supplements to, if not reduce the size of the gland, at least slow its growth. (He opted out on the use of dutasteride which would have shrunk the gland when he learned the side effects were loss of sexual prowess, a higher pitched voice and breast growth.) On the Internet, he found an ad for a prostate massager, which he bought and used regularly in the hopes that it would prevent a reoccurrence of the urine retention. He even went so far as to find a masseuse, Madam Orey, in Oneonta where, once a month, he would have the prostate massaged and relieved.

As he learned more about his problem the more he became convinced that "intelligent design" was a myth. Who, with any kind of intelligence would have designed a system by which a tube, necessary for a daily bodily function, passed through a structure that increased in size as a person aged? As an engineer, Jerry was appalled. He could also not help but think that maybe, after all, God was really a woman and this was Her way of extracting revenge.

His morning supplements taken and having checked his stock investments on the financial page of the <u>Star</u>, Jerry checked his calendar. In doing so, he also noticed that the date of Lawyer's funeral was the same day as the TCA, York meet. That also reminded him to give Tom a call to be sure arrangements for their trip to Pennsylvania were all set. Before he returned to his layout, he left a voicemail reminder for Tom.

— Chapter 4 —

GIVEN THEIR DIVERSE BACKGROUNDS, Tom being from an old established family whereas Jerry was a newcomer to Palatine County, they were not exactly friends. Although they both were members of the country club, this background was not enough to make them more than nodding acquaintances. However, quite by accident, they did find that they shared a common interest in toy trains. This "accident" came about when Jerry discovered there was another member of the Train Collectors Association living in Snyder's Corners and made a phone call to Tom. That was two years ago and they had been sharing the trip to York ever since.

In 1954, a group of sixty-eight men met in a barn in Yardley, Pennsylvania to discuss the state of their hobby. That hobby was toy trains. At a time when the real trains were diminishing in importance—especially on the passenger side—and the companies that made the replicas were sliding toward mediocrity, these men were concerned with preserving the integrity of the toy train hobby. This was especially true for those who found enjoyment and profit in collecting toy trains from the past. To this end, this group organized themselves into what was to become the Train Collectors Association (TCA). Joined that same year by a similar group on the West Coast, the TCA became, almost instantaneously, a national association.

While the stated purpose of the group was to preserve the toy train hobby, the underlying motive of many was to protect themselves from their fellow members. This was especially true when it came to the sale of the older, collectible items since some were on the market that had been forged, repaired with new parts but sold as originals, while many were being misrepresented as to either condition or manufacturing date. To this end, the TCA set up a system of a constantly evolving set of ten grading standards for toy trains relating to the condition and description of the item. (Later, when toy train catalogs and boxes were also deemed collectibles, a ten level grading standard was added for them.) To maintain this integrity the TCA became an arbitrator between members when dealing with the sale of trains and train related items to the point where, if found guilty of any kind of misrepresentation and unwilling to compensate the fellow member for this deception, a member could be expelled from the Association. In addition, in order for someone to join and to assure the honor of the organization, applicants had to be recommended, in writing, by two members in good standing who would attest to their honesty and reliability. While a large number of the members of TCA were just hobbyists who were interested in running their trains and building layouts either of their own or with other hobbyists, there was a distinct group of members whose sole interest was having a collection of rare and hard to find trains and adding to it.

Whatever the motivation, the initial group grew and multiplied. Incorporated in 1957 in Pennsylvania, by 1977 the IRS had granted TCA nonprofit status as an educational organization. Using this status, the Association built its national headquarters in Strasburg, Pennsylvania where, in the same year, it also built The National Toy Train Museum. To make the Association more locally accessible and easier to administrate, the TCA was broken into twenty divisions spread across the country. One of these divisions is the Eastern Division, which is headquartered in Pennsylvania and draws membership from part or all of the states of Pennsylvania, New York, New Jersey, Maryland, Delaware, Virginia and the District of Columbia.

For whatever reason, there is a high concentration of toy train enthusiasts in the northeastern United States. There are a number of explanations as to why this area is rife with toy train operators and collectors but a few stand out. The generally the most accepted one may be that this area is high the number of houses which are constructed over open cellars where trains can be run out of the way of the rest of the household. More likely it could be that, at one time, the area was home to some of the largest and most famous prototype railroads—New York Central, Pennsylvania Railroad, Baltimore and Ohio, Chesapeake and Ohio. Whatever the reason, couple these factors with the aging of the population, many of whom worked for these lines and/or were nostalgic for the good old days, and you have a prime area for modeling trains. Given this demographic, it is not hard to see why the TCA started here, why one of its more active divisions is located in this area and why it became home to one of the country's largest train meets.

Even before TCA's inception, members of hobby got together to exchange train items. Someone had a locomotive that no longer interested them. Someone wanted an especially rare item to fill out his collection. A member tired of a particular type of livery and wanted to trade it for that of another railroad line. A modeler was redoing his layout and had excess track or needed more track and did not want to buy it new. Older models of trains, rolling stock and accessories broke down and needed cannibalized parts from used items that belonged to someone else. For whatever reason, there were those who had something to get rid of and those who wanted to buy or trade for it. Often it was just an even swap, but in some cases, if it was an especially rare item, money exchanged hands.

Originally the swaps/sales meetings were between individual hobby members but gradually they became more formally organized and were scheduled once or twice a year within a particular club. But as the individual clubs became involved within the divisions of the TCA, the word got around through TCA publications about the better swap meets and these meets grew. Since the TCA now covered larger areas, individual clubs' swap meets now had to be scheduled at specific times and places to accommodate other groups and avoid conflict. In many cases it was better served to combine the smaller, individual club swap meets into a single, centralized divisional meet. As the organization's largest division and because it soon held the largest of these meets, the Eastern Division's meet grew to be a big enough size to need a central place to hold it. Since the epicenter of this division is at or near southern Pennsylvania, they settled on the city of York, Pennsylvania as the best site.

This city, some dozen or so miles south the state capitol, Harrisburg, and within easy driving distance of most of the larger cities in the northeast, is located in a rural area where farming is a major occupation. For that reason, the county built its fair grounds on the edge of the city to host an annual agricultural fair and expo complete with exhibits and horse races. Since this fair took only a week out of the ground's schedule it was not long before other organizations rented out the facility to put on shows of their own. Beginning in 1967, and for two weeks out of the year, once in April and the other in October, the Eastern Division took over the fair grounds.

As long as it was a swap meet and the commerce that took place transpired between members of what was an educational organization, the state tax department kept its nose out of it, even though the amounts of money exchanged could become large. In order to preserve this tax-free environment, the Eastern Division and TCA declared the meet a closed club event, open to members only. While TCA members, regardless of what division they belonged to, were eligible to attend, nonTCA members could attend only once in their lifetimes and then only if, during that one time, a member sponsored them. This made the meet very exclusive, desirable, and a big incentive for joining TCA.

The meet also developed in another way. While the TCA encompasses all scales and types of toy trains from the tiny Z-scale (1:220) to live steam, the York meet evolved into one that showcased primarily the 1:48, O-gauge trains and accessories. While there were some S-gauge (1:64) being sold to satisfy those who dabbled in this near O-gauge scale, the next larger size prevailed. In so doing, this meet drew the largest number of O-gauge collectors and operators in the country.

As news of the meet and the demographics of those who would attend began to spread through the hobby, more and more commercial vendors wanted to become involved. Since TCA membership was required for attending either as a buyer or seller, both hobbyists and those who sold to them joined with the specific purpose of gaining admittance to York. By and large, these new members had no interest in preserving their hobby except as it specifically affected them. Commercial sellers joined to make the market available to them. For those who collected trains or sold to collectors, the age-old adages of buy cheap/sell dear and may the best man win, figured into dealings. Now, rather than swapping items, many factory-fresh products were being sold at reduced (blow-out) prices by dealers that had regular brick and mortar stores as far away as Boston, Miami and Chicago. With this, those attending the meet were no longer just collectors, but "operators", hobbyists who ran their trains on layouts and wanted the newest items available. This meant that the manufacturers of trains and train related items set up displays to showcase their latest items and models of items to come. By 2000 Lionel and MTH had two of the largest commercial displays on the grounds and many innovations by train and accessory manufacturers made their initial appearance at this meet. The only fallout from this commercialization was that Pennsylvania's sales tax department began to take notice and required those professional vendors to charge tax. Many did if the sale was traceable, such as when a check or credit card was used, but most ignored this if it was a cash transaction. Most of those who were still hobby orientated overlooked this requirement completely.

Still the event grew in both sellers and attendance. By the nineteen nineties, the two dates for the York meet—generally the third Friday and Saturday of October and April and scheduled for at least three years in advance—were the biggest events on any train hobbyist's calendar and were attended by O-gauger's from all over the country. So many made it a biannual event that they would make their motel accommodations six months to a year in advance and then, once they had a room, regularly renew it six months ahead for the next meet. Trying to get a room within twenty miles of York during the week of the meet became impossible. It was not unknown for motel clerks to laugh in the phone at those trying to book a room at the last minute.

So large did the demand for items become that their sale soon spilled beyond the fair grounds and the two days reserved for it. Venders began setting up in motel rooms and parking lots as early as Monday and buyers flocked to them in ever-increasing numbers. These "Bandit" sales had the advantage of offering many bargains in new and slightly used items but had the disadvantage of not being sanctioned by the TCA. At least those items sold on the fair grounds, since the seller had to be a TCA member, had the backing of the Association and, if the buyer felt cheated in some way, there was some recourse. The Bandit meet buyers had to abide by caveat emptor.

Many were willing to take the chance; many were not. Either way, over twenty thousand members, with their kith and kin, showed up in York twice a year to buy, sell, and renew friendships with fellow hobbyists. If they were lucky, they might even run into Neil Young, Mandy Patinkin, or a CEO of a toy train company. York was the Mecca for toy train hobbyists, something they had to do at least once before they died. And once done, was done again and again.

This was the one an only time Jerry and Tom would set aside their differences and travel to Pennsylvania together. The TCA meet in York became their armistice.

— Chapter 5 —

AMY FINALLY RETURNED BILL'S call late on Thursday evening.

"Hi bro." She greeted him as soon as he picked up. "Sorry I haven't gotten back to you sooner but John seemed to have forgotten to give me the message." John was John Givens, Amy's live-in, Jamaican-born lover and the latest in a long line of these special friends.

"That's ok Sis. I was just worried that he didn't understand my message. With his patois it is tough to know if he gets things or not."

"Oh he understands ok, it is just that he never writes anything down so if we don't connect or he forgets I might not get messages."

"Well, are you going to the funeral or not?" Bill did not have lot of time to spend talking to Amy about her male friends.

"I guess so, if you're willing to pick me up." She did not sound enthusiastic but it would not have been like her if she did.

"Yeah, I figured on it. Mom and Pop seem to think they can make it with Pop driving so it'll be just us. I'll come down and get you about eight tomorrow morning."

"Oh God help the rest of the drivers. OK, I'll try to be ready."

"Try real hard, will you? I'd like to make the trip without having to break all the speed limits."

"You and your schedules. See you in the morning. Bye." There was a click on the other end to indicate the conversion was over.

****

Bill had grown up in Rhinebeck about an hour from New York City but had rarely ventured into "The City" except when out-of-town relatives wanted to go there. Consequently, he was not entirely at ease when driving in the city or the immediate suburbs. Since Amy, who loved the hustle and bustle of this environment, lived on the lower West Side, it meant that Bill had to overcome his fears and venture into Manhattan. He had made the trip several times before, so the route was at least familiar to him.

Fortunately, Amy was not only ready on time but was actually waiting on the curb, thus eliminating his need to find a parking place.

"Hi Sis." He had opened the passenger door to let her in, noting that she had on a dark dress but one that was hardly funeral attire—revealing as it did every curve of her five-foot, six-inch body. It was an especially warm day for October so she wore no outer clothing which served to further show off her figure. Bill could not help but notice it but, inasmuch as she was his sister—abet twelve years younger—he could not bring himself to think of her as "sexy". Rather he simply observed that she seemed especially youthful looking considering the life she had led since leaving college. The one exception was the set of her jaw which gave her a hard look, like life was okay but not really that great. Aside for that she was a tall, blond and a real looker. If anything, he attributed his sister's looks to good genes overcoming a poor lifestyle.

"Hi, yourself." She gave him a quick kiss, missing his cheek and getting an ear. She tossed her oversized pocketbook in the back and buckled herself in. "How you been?"

"Same old, same old. Kids are getting worse and the State is getting tougher. I'm looking forward to retirement more and more each day. You?"

"What's to tell? Not getting any younger but, considering the alternative, I guess I can't complain. Getting a little tired of John, but then, at my age I doubt I can do any better."

"Your age? Amy, you're twelve years younger than I, a mere child!" Bill loved to dig his sister about their age difference. Almost exactly a dozen years apart—both had birthdays in September, his was on the third and hers on the eighth—they liked to assume they were both products of New Years Eve celebrations.

"Hey that's right; you hit the big Five O this year! God, that means I'm getting close to be forty. My life's half over!" Amy laughed in a way that indicated she either did not really think so or did not care.

"Aw, if I were forty again, knowing what I know now...." He did not bring up the fact that his sister had forgotten his birthday, primarily because he had forgotten hers.

"Yeah, right. At forty you were still married to that hippy Phyllis. What became of her anyhow?

"Last I knew she was living on the West Coast someplace. She's finally remarried so I'm off the alimony payments at last."

"How about Chloe?"

"She's married, living in Seattle. I get a card at Christmas. Hey, if we are going to get caught up on exes, yours will fill in the conversation for the rest of the trip." Bill did not particularly care to talk about his ex-wife or daughter, the whole episode bringing back a lot of painful memories so he hoped this would end the conversation.

"True," Amy laughed. Then, falling silent, looked out the window.

By this time, having crossed the Tappan Zee Bridge, they were on the New York State Thruway so the scenery abruptly changed from urban to rural. Not only did this bridge and the Hudson River serve as a boundary line separating city from country, it also marked the point where the NYS Department of Transportation needed to do some maintenance.

The DOT, having an overabundance of orange cones and barrels, was using them to narrow the road to a single lane in advance of a work zone. This meant the traffic had to slow to a crawl until all three northbound lanes merged into one, so one could not go any faster than the slowest driver in line. Of course, too, it also meant that the drivers in the inner lanes took as long as possible to merge so there was a traffic jam at the merging point. It frosted Bill that these late mergers did not have foresight to get into line early and that the early mergers let them in line. It seemed to him that it made the traffic jam worse.

After ten miles and half an hour of this, the work zone was finally reached and consisted of three men standing on a bridge—two leaning on the railing, smoking, while the third was visually checking the structure. The pace immediately picked up once this bottleneck was passed.

They were through the tollbooth at Harriman and on Route 17 before Bill broke the silence.

"So, Uncle William passed away. Funny, I don't remember that much about him other than his store."

"Oh, I do." Amy made a face, the tone of her voice darkened and her jaw clinched further. "You never spent as much time with him as I did."

"That's right. You and Mom used to spend the whole summer up at Snyder's Corners, didn't you?"

"Yeah. Mom used to think she had to take care of her big brother and dragged me along for company. I swear, I spent most of my pre and early teen years in that one-horse town."

"Was it that bad?"

"Oh, you'll never know." Again, Amy fell silent but this time Bill sensed she was not looking at scenery.

****

The Gates and Sons Funeral Home in Snyder's Corners was not hard to find. Located on Main Street next to the Palatine National Bank, it was, if not at the center of town, at least in the busiest part of it. Bill managed to find a parking spot in the lot behind the bank and he and Amy walked over to the home. Their mother and father were waiting on the sidewalk just outside the entry.

"Billy and Amy!" Their mother spied them first—not surprising, given their father's eyesight. "I'm so glad you could make it. Uncle William would be so happy you could come."

Again Bill noticed that same "look" on Amy's face that he had seen in the car.

"Mother...Dad" was the only greeting she gave.

Both smiled at their daughter but said nothing.

"Sorry to have cut it so close Mom but there was construction on the Thruway." It was nine-fifty. Bill gave his mother a hug and smiled at his father who nodded in recognition.

"Well, Billy, you should have allowed for that, there is always construction on the Thruway someplace. It's your toll money at work, after all." His mother always seemed to have to admonish him for something. "Let's get inside, shall we?" She was nearly pushing her husband into the parlor itself.

They were met at the door by the funeral director, a young man with a permanent smile etched on his face and a sad demeanor. He introduced himself as Steve Gates the funeral director. His mother introduced herself as the sister of the deceased and then went about making introductions of her husband, Bill and Amy. Gates, after offering his condolences, ushered them to the front where they made a rapid trip past the open casket—Bill hardly recognized the body lying there—and on to front seats. He could not help but notice, however, that Amy did not look at all.

As he turned to sit down, Bill made a quick glance around the room to check the size and composition of the crowd. It was not large, maybe a dozen people and Bill assumed, correctly, that the younger ones, mostly women, were from the nursing home. Considering Uncle William's age and the fact that he had not been in business for some twenty years, most of those who knew him had either died or simply forgotten. There was one rather distinguished gentleman sitting near the back who did not seem like he belonged. When Bill caught the man's eye, the man nodded at him.

The service, done by the local Lutheran minister, was, blessedly, brief. Since there were no pallbearers, Uncle William's casket was wheeled out of the room on a gurney and placed in the hearse for the trip to the cemetery. The only cars in the procession were Bill's, his father's and a third, a big Lincoln Town Car that Bill could not place.

Uncle William, because he never married, was to be interred in the family plot amongst all the rest of the Lawyers, their kith and kin. While waiting for that part of the rites, Bill took the time to glance around at the tombstones, reading names and dates. He could not help but notice that his mother's half of his family had a plot in the older, pre1850, part of the cemetery. Many of the dates went back to the early eighteen hundreds. (The Weavers were considered newcomers so their burial plots were relegated to the other side or "new" part of the cemetery.) The Lawyer's plot was surrounded by big trees and contained monuments that showed marked signs of erosion with some names and dates nearly lost to weathering. There were also surrounding plots of similar age that contained the remains of other, original families in the area. Palatine names abounded—they had to cross the Bisignani family plot to get to the Lawyer's. Without realizing it, Bill began to arithmetically check the birth/death dates on some his ancestor's stones and could not help but note there seemed to be a longevity gene in the family. Most of his relatives seemed to have lasted well into their late eighties. He wondered it the same was in store for him.

The "Ashes to Ashes" part of the ceremony complete and, with Uncle William's casket lowered out of sight; Bill took Amy's arm to help negotiate the sunken gravesites on the way back to the car. With her seated in his car, he started around to the driver's side when a hand on his shoulder restrained him.

"William Weaver, I presume?" Bill turned to see the man who had nodded at him in the funeral home. "I am Sam Aaronson of Aaronson, Aaronson and Bernstein—your uncle's law firm. I wanted to get to you sooner but you weren't available before the service. "

"Yeah, we were late—traffic." Bill was taken aback.

"Right, traffic up from The City is a bitch. Your toll money at work." The lawyer smiled. "I assume the young lady with you is your sister, Amy."

"Yes, would you like to speak with her?"

"Not now but I am in charge of your uncle's will. It will be read in our office as soon as you and she can get there—you're both mentioned in it. We're easy to find, right across from the Post Office, next to the Snyder's Corners Tavern."

"Ok." Bill was a bit surprised at this news and not sure how he should react. "We're going directly back to town so should be there in a few minutes. "

"That will be fine. See you there then." The lawyer shook Bill's hand, turned and walked to the Town Car—it beeped to let him know it was open and ready.

"Should I bring my parents too?" Bill called just before the Lincoln's door closed.

"You can" was the reply "although they aren't mentioned."

Puzzled, Bill got in to his car.

"Who was that?"

"Uncle William's lawyer. Wants us to come to his office now for the reading of Uncle William's will. Says we're both mentioned in it."

"Well, I'll be damned." There was that "look" again.

"One thing that puzzles me though."

"What's that?"

"He said neither Mom nor Pop is in the will."

"Well I'll be God Damned."

****

Bill managed to overtake his parents before they got back to town and, after much gesturing got his father to pull over so they could talk. Both agreed to follow him to the lawyer's office for the reading of Uncle William's will. Bill did not tell them that neither was mentioned in it.

The law offices of Aaronson, Aaronson and Bernstein were in an old Italianate house next to the Snyder's Corners Tavern. Like the Tavern next door, this house dated back to the last real building boom in Snyder's Corners in the mid eighteen eighties. Unlike most of the buildings from the era, this one had been well taken care of and was one of the better specimens of its type in the area. The law offices took up the whole of the lower floor of the building, the upper story reserved for some of the better apartments in town.

The receptionist showed the Weaver family into Sam Aaronson's office and he, once he had greeted everyone and shaken both Bill and his father's hand, found seats for them.

Not being someone to take up people's time—or his own, for that matter—with niceties, Sam got right down to business.

"Your Uncle William directed that our firm be responsible for caring for his last will and testament, this being dictated to us and signed back in nineteen eighty-nine." The lawyer spoke directly to Amy and Bill, ignoring their parents who neither noticed this slight nor seemed to mind. "I will read it as dictated and signed."

"I, William Augustus Lawyer, being of sound mind and body do this day of August twenty third, nineteen eighty-nine, bequeath, to be divided equally, all my property and assets to my niece, Amy nee

Weaver, and nephew, William Weaver. I also direct that, should either of these persons die before my passing, then the entire estate shall go to the remaining heir. In the event they have both died, the assets shall be sold at auction and the money given to the Palatine County Republican Party. "

The lawyer placed the will on the desk and looked at first Amy—seemingly for the first time to take note of her dress—and then at Bill. "That is the good news. The bad news is, I am afraid, that his property and assets are not as extensive as they were in nineteen eighty-nine. Since your uncle was on Medicaid, New York State insisted that his assets and savings be liquidated and used for his care before he was able to qualify for aid. That included the sale of the family home", for the first time Sam acknowledged Bill's parents, "as well as all his investments. However—now some good news—he had placed his former business and the building housing it in an irrevocable trust, which was not considered his personal property. As such, that cannot be taken by the State but, upon his death can be passed on to his named heirs. In short, you two have inherited the building that housed his store and what contents remain inside."

Bill glanced sideways at Amy. Her face was a blank.

"Now", the lawyer continued, "the lower part of the building had been converted into two apartments before your uncle went into the nursing home. The money for the rent of these apartments went partly to pay the loan he took out to remodel the building, partly to pay the taxes on the building, and the remainder to the trust. The firm of Aaronson, Aaronson and Bernstein has also taken a fee from these rents to manage this fund as well as the building. You will find that the loan had been repaid several years ago and, even with the deduction of these payments, this fund has accrued to fifty thousand dollars and some change. There is a complete breakdown of these payments and fees in this folder if you wish to have your accountant or lawyer check them. Here are copies of what has transpired. " Sam slid a file folder across the desk in the general direction of Bill.

Bill, reached out for the folder, took it, but did not open it. His mind was numb. He again glanced at his sister. Her demeanor had not change but he thought he detected a tear glistening in the corner of her eye.

"Thank you. I don't have either an accountant or a lawyer but I am sure you have done an honest job." This was all that Bill could think to say.

Meantime he was thinking: *Hell, I'm a school teacher. Why for God's sake, would I need an accountant? As far as a lawyer was concerned, I've managed to stay away from those since my divorce.* Then he though *Damn, I'm sure glad both Amy and I are still alive. I'd have hated for that fifty thousand to go to the Republicans.*

"I would suggest you might want to take a look at your new property. Right now only one of the apartments on the lower floor is rented but there have been several inquiries concerning the other. On the other hand, the upper story is pretty much like it was when your uncle closed the store. I've never been up there but I'm told it was used for storage even before the store closed. I'm sure there are a lot of odds and ends of stock left from the store. You might want to check it out." The lawyer held out a key. "This is for the back stairway."

Bill took the key and managed another "Thanks"

"Do you need directions to the store?"

"No, I think I can remember how to get there. Thank you again." Bill started to rise. "Is there anything else you need us for?"

"Well there are papers to be signed, we will need to transfer the money into accounts for both of you and you will have to file a deed with the county but that can be taken care of either next week or through the mail. If you'd like to check your property, I will understand." Sam Aaronson rose from behind the desk and walked to Bill, offering his hand.

Bill shook the lawyer's hand but Amy, still seated, neither said a word nor followed his lead.

"Are you alright?" Bill half knelt in front of her and looked directly into her eyes.

"Yes, just stunned, I guess." Her voice was low, almost little girl-like. Slowly she gathered herself and rose. "Thank you," she finally said in the general direction of the lawyer and, turning on her heels, walked out of the office.

Noting that the lawyer was checking her ass as she left his office, Bill hung back to help his parent to their feet.

"Congratulations, Billy, it seems this was a lucky day for you." His mother smiled at him with no disappointment in either her face or voice.

"Yes," his father added, "seems like you finally have some money in the bank."

"But," inquired Bill, "there was nothing for you, Mother, aren't you disappointed?"

"Not in the least." She smiled, "We both knew what your Uncle William wanted to do with his money. He had told me a long time ago that you, children, would get what was left."

"Then you knew what was going to happen?" Bill was still stunned.

"Of course, Dear, now make good use of it." She took her husband's arm and half leaning on it and half guiding her husband, walked out of the lawyer's office. "Now you and Amy had best be getting over to Uncle William's old store to see what it is you inherited. Your father and I will take one swing around by the old house then will be getting back to Rhinebeck. It is nearly noon now and we want to be home before dark."

Bill could not help but think: *Let's see, it's a little over one hundred miles. The sun sets around five. You should just make it in time.*

Smiling he said, "Okay, drive safely Pop."

They turned and waved as they headed for their car. Bill waved back.

Once outside, Bill looked for Amy. She was no place in sight.

It took him a little bit of time to locate her. He found her sitting on a bar stool in the Tavern, a heavy glass of dark liquor in front of her. She was the only patron.

"Scotch and water", She said when she caught him staring. "Since I just inherited a lot of money, I bought a good stiff one. God knows, I can use it. Join me?"

"God, Sis, it's not even quite noon."

"All the more reason. Have one with me then we can check out old Uncle William's gift to us."

Reluctantly Bill pulled up a stool. He ordered a bottle of beer.

— Chapter 6 —

SEAN, "BOOMBOOM", CLEARY WAS in the money. Last week he had made a big sale on eBay and, the check having cleared, had added another eight hundred dollars and change to his bank account. The money had not been earned by honest means.

BoomBoom's business actually got started five years ago completely by accident. Walking down the street near his home in North Bergen, New Jersey, he noticed a cardboard box lying next to the curb. At loose ends and with nothing better to do, he picked up the box and discovered it to contain half a dozen of the latest model of Sony's Playstation. Apparently some employee of a delivery service had inadvertently left the door on the back of their truck ajar and lost the package—it was addressed to an electronics outlet out on Route 17. Not being one to look a gift horse in the mouth and in complete agreement with the adage that finders were keepers, BoomBoom carried the carton back to his mother's house—where he still lived—and to his room.

Now, BoomBoom had always wanted a Playstation but he surely did not need all six. In addition, these players needed game cartridges, something he could not afford, given that he was at the time an unemployed, high school dropout who had been recently fired from his job of emptying garbage cans at McDonald's. He first considered trying to sell the extra game consoles to guys he knew on the street but rejected that idea as one where he would either get ripped off or turned in by some narc. Despite his half-Irish ancestry, BoomBoom, was, at slightly less than five-foot six and one hundred-forty pounds, not a fighter. He had survived growing up in a gang infested environment by carefully avoiding any conflict. He found early in his school career that, when confronted with a bully or gang member, his best defense was compliance. While it served him well as he avoided beatings, he often ended up on the short end of the confrontation either losing his lunch money, some prized article or his dignity. For this reason he was not sure how he should proceed in divesting himself of these articles at a profit.

While in the midst of this quandary, BoomBoom was startled to hear his mother shout "Yes!" from downstairs. Checking to see what caused this outburst, BoomBoom, went down to the living room to see his mother sitting in front of her computer, a picture of a ceramic poodle on the screen.

"What's going on?"

"You see this?" His mother pointed to the image on the screen. "I just won it on eBay. Won't it be nice with the rest of those?" His mother indicated a bric-a-brac shelf full of ceramic and stuffed poodles of various sizes, shapes and colors.

"Yeah, sure." There was not a lot of enthusiasm in BoomBoom's voice.

Then it hit him. *I can sell those extra Playstations on eBay.* So later that day, after his mother left for her waitress job, BoomBoom opened an account on eBay and successfully put up the first Playstation for bid. Five years later, he had his own apartment, a car and money in the bank.

He also could no longer depend on finding stuff on the street. He stole it.

Although BoomBoom's initial product arrived quite by accident, the ease at which he made that first sale convinced him that he needed more stock and quickly. He also realized he could not rely on finding items lying in the street. This meant he had to find another source for new merchandise. Fortunately, there were plenty of delivery trucks running around the streets of Northern New Jersey, many unlocked and unguarded, which made for easy pickings. In addition, as BoomBoom was quick to discover, all too often drivers were in too much of a hurry to wait for signatures or to see if the recipient was around to take delivery of packages. This latter occurrence proved especially fruitful in the two months leading up to Christmas when there were a lot of deliveries to be made and the companies hired temporary workers. This made for easy pickings for someone who was not concerned about the kind of items in the parcels. It was in such a package, collected from the front foyer of an apartment house in Paramus, that BoomBoom obtained his first electric train, a Lionel F-3 diesel with TMCC.

When he opened the package and saw the contents, he did not know he had stumbled on anything of any worth. It was, after all, a toy. However, once he went to eBay and checked on similar items being offered, he was surprised to find that, not only were these items selling, but the prices were high. He was pretty sure he lucked into a winner.

Now just because BoomBoom had dropped out of high school it did not mean he was lacking in street smarts. He instinctively knew that the one thing that would expose him would be greed. He had known enough guys on the street that had good things going for them only to be undone when they got greedy and overreached themselves. He was determined not to let it happen to him. Therefore, he realized that when selling these items on eBay, he needed to be sure to keep prices within certain limits to avoid suspicion. To do this, he kept an eye on similar items and then offered his at an initial price a bit lower than the competition. Occasionally he would just start items for a penny—usually with excellent results—or put a minimum selling price near to the possible dealer cost to avoid detection. Regardless of which technique he used, he always seemed to get excellent prices for his stock—not that it made any difference since he had nothing invested in the first place.

He also refused to take anyone into his confidence. Again, he had an instinctive feeling that he would have a better chance of success with less chance of being discovered if he avoided any kind of partnership. This also kept his operating costs low since he did not have to share.

Because of this low overhead—he stored the items for sale in a spare room of his apartment or his mother's empty garage—and since the initial cost was nil, he was able to sell items cheaper than most of the competition. He was always careful not to overcharge for shipping by keeping this cost to the lower limit of what the shipping charges actually cost. Shipping boxes were not a problem since he usually just used the ones the product came in—with the original addressee's name removed, of course. If there was any complaint regarding either the item or its condition by the bidder, BoomBoom always replaced it if he had another like it or refunded money if he did not. There were never any questions asked and he made sure his bidders were completely satisfied. He prided himself in having one-hundred percent positive feedback. This made him an excellent eBay seller and because he moved a lot of items, it was not long before he achieved Power Seller ranking.

Initially, as might be expected, he offered a variety of merchandise but he found that his best sellers were either small electronic devices or electric train items. With this in mind, it did not take him long to discover that the best places to pilfer both kinds of these items where at trade and/or hobby shows where both old and new items were on display and sold. The sponsors of these shows hired a lot of temporary workers to help sellers setup and unload/load merchandise, some of which was delivered to the site before the actual show was opened. In addition, the venders at these shows rarely knew until well after they got back home which of their unsold items were missing. All of this made it easy to walk off with cartons of merchandise without detection. Since it was no longer necessary to resupply by hit or miss "found" deliveries, it was not long before BoomBoom began to specialize in these items. He fostered this specialization by traveling around the Northeast attending a number of electronic and train shows. To make moving items easier and give himself a legitimate reason for being there, he purchased a small, enclosed trailer that he pulled behind his car on which he alternated magnetic signs which either read Bergen Electronics or Bergen Trains—depending on the type of show. This trailer was empty when he arrived at the show but rode considerably lower on the way back.

It was not long too before he joined the TCA.

That first locomotive had sold so quickly and at such a high final bid that it piqued BoomBoom's interest in similar items. As he monitored bidding on locomotives, train cars, accessories, track and parts, it occurred to him that the people who were interested in these things not only had money to spend but also were willing to part with it in ridiculous amounts for the right item. Since some of the higher priced items seemed to be preowned and/or old, it caused him to do some research into these kinds of products. This led him to discover the market for train collectibles. Expanding this research he eventually discovered the Train Collectors Association and shortly thereafter he learned about York. Once he heard about it, he knew it was going to be a mother lode if he could just figure out how to get into the show.

For someone with no scruples, it did not prove all that difficult. Since to get into the meet itself, one had to be a member of TCA, he only had to overcome that obstacle. As somebody who was used to picking up objects of value that were lying around, it did not prove to be too complicated. Using the newfound information he had gleaned from his Internet research, he hung around the local hobby shops that sold train items—some of which had been left outside too long and ended up in his mother's garage—and talked to the clerks and customers. It did not take him long to find and befriend several hobbyists who were members of TCA. Since these TCA members were anxious to recruit new enthusiasts into their hobby, it was not hard for BoomBoom to get them to loan him a few of their magazines, including their TCA publications. He easily copied the members' names and membership numbers from the mailing labels and by carefully forging their signatures, used two to recommend him for membership. As he suspected, the organization, eager for new membership, never checked these recommendations coming from his area of New Jersey. Fifty dollars and a year later, BoomBoom was a full-fledged member with his own identification number—one that he added to his site when selling train items on eBay. That next spring BoomBoom had free access to the York Fair Grounds.

This made his life easier and increased his access to more stock. While those professional vendors who had their own shops were more alert to shoplifting, it was easy to rip them off either early or late when they set up or tore down. It was the amateurs who sold used items that could be simply distracted and, before they refocused their attention, relieved of an item or two. Using this technique, BoomBoom came into possession of a large quantity of collectible items and spare parts. While this was good, it also caused him some consternation since he was afraid, since many of the items were rare, that, if he offered these items on eBay someone might become suspicious.

Fortunately, he found a way around this: direct sales. Hanging out at the York meet either at the fair grounds or at the Bandit sales prior to the first day, he met a number of collectors of really rare items. It did not take him long to learn that some of these men's passion for collecting certain trains and train related items went beyond the bounds of legality. In short, if they wanted it badly enough, they did not care where the item came from as long as it was available and the price was right. BoomBoom was soon able to satisfy this faction of the hobby. That was why at two-thirty in the afternoon on the third Friday of October he was in York, Pennsylvania to meet up with a couple of possible buyers

He checked out a rear booth of the Round the Clock Diner as he came in the door and was glad to see his clients had not gotten there ahead of him. BoomBoom liked to be punctual even to the point of being early. It gave him a chance to see who was there and get a good seat where he could see his customers and position himself so he could hear them well.

BoomBoom had one physical problem; he was hard of hearing in one ear. As a teenager, he had earned his nickname from the fact that his constant companion was a SONY boom box that rode on his left shoulder like an attached limb. He kept it cranked up so loud that people knew he was in the neighborhood before actually laying eyes on him. One day a five-year old girl who lived across the street yelled out "Here comes the Boom Boom." From that day forward Sean Cleary became BoomBoom to everyone he knew, even to the point that he signed his name that way.

The loud music had not left him unscathed. Gradually he noticed he had to crank the volume up higher and higher on the box to hear it. At the same time, he noticed that he was having a harder time hearing things coming at him from his left side. The verdict was delivered when he applied for a factory job shortly after quitting high school and he was required to take the first physical of his life. The application was turned down since his hearing was such that the company would not hire him with this pre-existing condition fearing that later in life he would run up the company's medical insurance for treatment of his hearing loss. At the time, it did not bother BoomBoom—he was young and bulletproof—but as he outgrew his teens, he became more aware that it was causing him difficulties. Before long, he bought a hearing aid using some of his profits from his business in an attempt to overcome this handicap.

It helped but it was not perfect. Often he could overhear conversations that he had no interest in while being unable to hear those people close to him. At other times, extraneous noise, such as elevator music, drowned out parts of conversations. Then the aid would, for no apparent reason, whistle in his ear. This annoying feedback seemed to happen when he was concentrating on some job like boosting a box of items off a loading dock, and it not only distracted him but made it impossible to hear if someone was sneaking up on him. He even feared that it was loud enough that someone else might hear it. Finally, the damn aid had the nasty habit of using up batteries just when he needed it most. For this reason, he always kept a package of spares in his car, his bedroom, on the shelf next to his computer and in his wallet. Today he wanted to be sure he heard everything, so had put in a new battery just before leaving his motel room for the diner.

He ordered a cup of coffee and a piece of pie from the waitress and waited. He did not know too much about either of these men except they were a couple of old geezers from somewhere in upstate New York that he had come to know through dealings at York. Since there were no electronic or train shows in that area, it was a place where BoomBoom had never been nor did he care to go. Being strictly a city boy, the woods and things that lived in them scared the hell out of him. All he knew was that one of these guys was a big collector and into prewar Lionel stuff. The other was more of an operator and into MTH. Both probably had more trains than anyone really needed but they also had a lot of money and were more than willing to spend it for the right stuff. BoomBoom was more than happy to be of assistance to them.

BoomBoom's coffee had just hit the right temperature to make it drinkable when Thomas Bisignani and Jerry Van Virden came in the door of the diner. Because of his hearing loss, BoomBoom relied more on his eyesight so he noticed the two men before they spotted him. He waved a greeting to Jerry and Tom. They acknowledged the greeting and joined him at the back booth.

— Chapter 7 —

IT WAS ABOUT AN hour and a couple of beers/scotches later when Amy and Bill emerged from the Tavern into the October afternoon sunlight. Although it had been over thirty-five years since he had been there, Bill had no problem locating the building that had housed Uncle William's store at 23 Main Street. There was a parking place in the alley next to it and the key that Aaronson had given him worked neatly in the lock for the back door. The backstairs was unlit but Bill found a light switch near the door and, miraculously the lights worked, not only on the stairs but also in the room above.

"Geeze!" Bill exclaimed when they topped the stairs into what had been the storage room. "Aaronson said he'd never been here. It looks like nobody has for a few years."

The middle of the room was filled with canvas covered piles while along the walls were shelves, some empty; others holding odds and ends of merchandise. A thick layer of dust covered everything; some undoubtedly had come from the construction done when converting the first floor into apartments, the rest having just settled due to inactivity. As the two siblings entered the room it caused enough air movement so that dust motes rose into the air, reflecting in the shafts of sunlight that entered through the holes in the newspapers that covered the west-facing windows.

Bill went to the nearest pile and pulled the canvas off it sending more dust skyward. He sneezed. Underneath were boxes of nails and screws, carefully arranged as to size and many in unopened cartons. Amy, following her brother's lead, went to another pile and uncovered several unopened cartons of paint. Gradually, they went around the room and uncovered more piles of more unsold hardware store merchandise. It was like a huge treasure hunt where paint, putty, nails, rope and the like, were the pots of gold. Once they got to the shelves, they discovered bigger things: saws, files, various other hand tools, most in their original packages, sometimes a group of a dozen or more, but often just single items. Finally, it was Bill who reached a single stack of goods at the furthest point in the room from the stairs. It was covered with a thicker layer of dust and, from all appearances had been there the longest. Pulling the canvas off, he exposed a cache of toys

Several GI Joes, Barbies and Kens, a couple of boxes of Dinky Super Trucks, and games, all in their original boxes, were neatly stacked under this last tarp. Amy, who was following close behind, reached in and picked up a Barbie in its original package. She took it over near the window where she pulled the cover of newspaper off so more light came in and she could get a better look.

"I would have loved to have this when I was ten." She held the doll to the light, turning it to take in the details.

Bill looked up from where he was about to pick up a large mailing package that was at the absolute bottom of the heap to see his sister silhouetted in the light. *Damn*, he thought, *I can see through that dress.* Rising to his feet, he took off his suit jacket and held it to Amy.

"Here, Sis, if you're going to stand like that, wrap this around your waist. "

"Sorry, Brother, am I embarrassing you?" Laughing, she took the jacket and tied the sleeves around her hips, blocking the sunlight.

"Not embarrassed, exactly. But I just didn't need to know you weren't wearing any underwear." He returned her smile, then went back to the package he had been about to pick up off the floor.

It was an unopened mailing carton addressed to his uncle and, to judge from the color and amount of dust, it had been there a long time. The return address was the Lionel Corp in Irvington New Jersey. First, he noticed that neither address had a zip code. Checking further, he found a dated postmark: April 30, 1929.

"Holy shit!"

"What?" Amy, still holding the doll, looked over at Bill.

"This sucker is really old." He held the package out for Amy to see. "It was mailed over seventy-six years ago."

"What is it?" Amy carefully picked her way past a carton of interior paint to get a closer look.

"Judging from the return address, I'd say something to do with Lionel trains." He handed Amy the package so she could get a better look.

"Oh!" It was heavier than she had anticipated and she almost dropped it. Bill reached out to intercept it before it hit the floor, but Amy recovered her grip and brought the package up to where she could read it. "Do you suppose whatever is in here is worth anything?"

"Oh, I imagine all this stuff is, especially the toys in unopened boxes. There is a guy I teach with that collects action figures and he tells me some of them are worth a mint. Assuming what is in these packages hasn't been tampered with, they may be valuable. Who knows?"

"How could we tell?" Amy handed the package back to Bill, who carefully placed in on the floor.

"Well, John Carson, he's the guy that buys and sells action figures, does most of his dealing on eBay. Maybe one of us should go online and see if there is anything like it being offered."

"It'll have to be you, I don't have a computer."

"Neither do I but maybe I could get John or someone else at school to do it for me."

"Hey wait a minute, come to think of it, Clare, the gal that works with me is always buying stuff on eBay, maybe she could help. In fact, I think her son is some sorta eBay seller. She talks all the time about how he makes all these big sales. Apparently, it is his sole source of income and he does well at it. I could ask her."

"Sounds like a good idea but why don't you wait until I check with John? In the meantime, what are we going to do with this stuff?" Bill's hand swept around the room and its piles of dust covered merchandise.

"I don't see any reason why it can't stay here. Hell, it's been here since before the place closed twenty-some years ago and no harm's come to it. Sure as hell all of this stuff won't fit in your car and, even if it did, I doubt either of us has room to store it."

"You're probably right. Maybe we should go back to Aaronson and tell him about it though. Let him keep an eye on it for us." Bill picked up the Lionel package and put it under his arm. It left a streak of dust on his shirt. "I am taking this though."

"What ever floats your boat." Amy looked around the room. "It looks like we've been through everything and I feel gritty. Let's get the hell out of here." Without thinking, she put the Barbie in the pocket of Bill's jacket as she handed it back to him.

Little did Bill know, but that toy train under his arm was about to change his and Amy's life in a profoundly interesting and dangerous way

****

The receptionist in the law office told them that Sam Aaronson had left for the weekend but that she expected him in first thing on Monday morning. Bill said that he would call but also told her that they were leaving all the stuff in the store's storage area that they would like watched. The receptionist said that would be taken care of.

"Well, now what? Back to the City?" Bill was standing by the car.

"I'm hungry. Are you?"

"I could eat."

"It used to be the Tavern put out a fairly good hamburger plate." Amy motioned in the general direction of the building next door. "Want to give it a try?"

"Ok, there's nothing but diners between here and the Thruway anyhow." Bill took off his jacket, laid it on the back seat and locked his car. "By the way, how do you know about the Tavern's hamburgers?"

"I used to come in here once in a while." Amy was already up the step to the side porch door. It led directly into the bar.

Puzzled, Bill followed. Then it occurred to him: *Now what was she doing in a place like this? There's a new thing I've just learned about my sister.*

After a silent dinner of an excellent burger washed down with a beer, Bill was ready for the trip back. He noticed his sister continued on the scotch, but this time it was neat. He got the feeling from the way she was hitting the booze and her quiet demeanor that something was eating at her. Having no clue as to what it was, he decided to wait until she was ready to tell him—assuming it ever happened. Even during the few years their lives at home overlapped, they were not the kind of siblings that shared secrets and there was no reason to expect it would happen now.

The silence continued on the drive down route 618 until it hooked up with Route 17. Once on the four-lane Bill glanced over at his sister. She was leaning against the door, looking at the scenery passing by.

"Tired?" He would see if he could draw her out of her mood a little.

"Not especially. Just thinking." She turned toward him; her voice was low, almost childlike. .

"What's up Sis? You've been acting odd at times all day. Could it be that Uncle William's funeral has you down?"

"Hardly!" She said it with such force that it caught Bill by surprise, causing him to take his eyes off the road to look over at her. "Actually the reason I came along was to makes sure that asshole was really dead."

"What?" This sentiment caught Bill completely off guard.

"Yeah, if you only knew, we're well rid of him. Maybe one of those aides who were at the funeral actually smothered him with a pillow. Wouldn't have been a bad idea."

"What?" Bill felt a twinge in the pit of his stomach as if he was about to hear something he did not want to know. "What's going on?"

He looked out the windshield, spotted a sign for a rest area coming up in a mile. "Ok, I'm going to pull over up ahead. Damn it. I want to know what in hell you're talking about."

"Ok, I guess its time you knew." Amy's voice was tiny again.

There was a couple with their dog in the designated dog walk only area between the highway and the parking area, otherwise the lot was empty when Bill pulled in. He purposely parked a couple of slots away from the restroom area and the other car. He shut off the motor and turned to his sister.

"Ok, spill it. I want to know what in hell is going on with you." He had turned where he could see his sister's face in the fading light.

Amy turned to her brother, lowered her eyes and began in that little girl's voice.

"You remember when Mom and I used to come up to visit Uncle William?"

Bill nodded. "Yeah, vaguely. It was mostly after I had graduated from high school and had gone on to college. You and she would go up so Mom could take care of him. You stayed all summer. What were you, about twelve?"

"I was ten when we first started and fourteen when I stopped."

"I remember that, it was the summer before I married Phyllis. I also remember there was a problem. You disappeared for most of the summer. What was that all about?"

"I'll get to that but there is something that has to be told first." Amy looked straight at Bill. "From the time I was ten until I was thirteen Uncle William use to use me."

"What!? Use you? You mean sexually?"

"Sort of. He did this thing."

"Thing? God, Sis, he didn't screw you did he?" Bill could feel the heat rising in his voice.

"No, nothing like that. Actually he never touched me."

"Then what was his 'Thing'"?"

"He masturbated in front of me."

"Oh shit! That must have been awful!"

"Worse still, he made me masturbate myself while he did it."

"Oh Jesus!" Bill was not sure but that he thought for a moment he was going to be physically ill. Repressing this urge he reached over and touched his sister's arm in a gesture he hoped would reassure her.

"Yeah. The trouble was I got so I liked it. If you remember, I matured early. I had boobs by the time I was eleven and began menstruating right about that time too. It was thrilling for me to do stuff like that, especially in front of someone. I guess it turned me on too." She did not acknowledge his touch, but did not move her arm away either.

"What about Mom? What was she doing while all this was going on?" Bill got this mental picture of his uncle and his sister and immediately wiped it from his mind. "Did she know about this?"

"I never told her. I don't know if I was afraid to or just afraid she'd make me stop." Amy was staring at her brother, her eyes clear, searching his face for any sign of what he might be thinking. "Funny thing though."

"What?"

"I think she knew. Later, when I went over everything in my mind, I not only think she knew what was going on but actually approved."

"Approved? What, approved of her daughter being molested by her brother?"

"Yeah, I think he had done the same thing to her over the years. She was just glad he was doing it with someone else to be rid of him."

"You can't be serious."

"Bill, I'm very serious. I'm sure that's the way it happened."

"Well, at least that explains why you and Mom don't get along very well."

"That's part of it."

"There's more?" What he had heard so far was more than he could digest at this point.

"Yeah, the part where I disappeared." Again, she looked at her brother. "Ready to hear it?" There was a hint of a smile in her voice.

"Might as well. Don't tell me it gets worse." He sat back on the seat, ready for worst.

"Well when I got to be about thirteen I began to realize what was going on wasn't a good thing. While I never discussed it with my girlfriends back home or anything, I sensed what I was doing was, somehow, wrong. I think too this was about the time I realized Mom was, if not in on it, at least knew what was happening. So when we went up to Uncle William's that summer, I started sneaking away from the house as soon as Uncle William came home from work. Some days I'd wander around in the woods near town but mostly I'd hang out in the evenings at the Tavern. I'd try not to return until they were both in bed. Sometimes I didn't get back until morning."

"Ok, now the hamburger thing makes sense but, hell Sis, you were only a kid."

"Yeah, but remember I was mature for my age and the guy that tended bar there didn't seem to mind."

"You drank?"

"Oh hell yes! Not a lot, just a beer here and there. I got so I could hold it pretty well." She looked up at him and smiled. "That's where I developed my taste for scotch, too."

"Well at least you had good taste and weren't a lush." Bill smiled back, hoping he was reassuring.

"I did that for two summers. That last summer is when I met Tom"

"Tom? Tom who?"

"No need to know his last name, there isn't any reason you need to know anyway. Besides, we never used last names anyway; I was just 'Amy', although I knew his and, I'm sure he knew mine. He was an older guy, maybe in his mid to late forties. He treated me well and I liked the attention. Something I learned from Uncle William, I guess."

"Late forties? Back when you were in your teens? Hell that would have made him just a little younger than Pop."

"Yeah, I guess so but I never thought of it that way. Besides this guy worked outside and was in great shape. Could have passed for early thirties, maybe even twenties. At any rate, that summer before you were married, I shacked up with him all summer."

"You what?"

" Had an affair."

"An affair? Your call that an affair? Hell, Sis, it was statutory rape— you were what, fourteen?"

"It was an affair, damn it!" Although the light had faded to the point where he could make out her facial expression, Bill could tell she was pouting. "I played house with this guy all summer. It was fun. He had one of those big satellite dishes so I'd lie around all day watching TV while he was at work, maybe drink a little. He'd come home make me supper then we'd go to bed."

"Shit, Sis, what would have happened if you got pregnant for Christ sake?" Bill realized he was madder about some guy shacking up with his sister than the fact that his uncle, maybe with his mother's compliance, had started the whole thing.

"There was nothing to worry about; he told me that he'd had a vasectomy. Besides, he was well connected in town, so nobody was going to bother him even if they knew what was going on. Like I said, he took good care of me. Some nights we'd go to Oneonta to a movie, sometimes he'd buy me things. I still have a sterling silver brooch with diamonds that he bought home from one of his overseas trips."

"And what was Mom doing all this time?"

"Oh, I'm sure she knew where I was but she seemed to ignore it. I never went back to Uncle William's again after that summer though. In fact, I didn't hang around home much at all after that summer. I was in high school by then and kind of wild. Most nights I just hung out with friends until it was time to go to school; slept over at my girl friends' houses and stuff. Mom never asked questions and Pop, well, Pop was Pop—clueless. As soon as I graduated, I got out of town. You probably don't remember because you were gone by then."

"How about this Tom?"

"As I said, I never went back to Uncle William's. In fact, this is the first time I've been in Snyder's Corners since that summer. As far as Tom is concerned, he would be in his seventies by now. Maybe dead. If not, he's probably forgotten me."

"Why didn't you tell me before this?"

"Hell, you were never around. Besides, you were the fair-haired boy. You were named after Uncle William, for Christ sake. There was no way I was going to tell you. Besides it turned out okay."

What do you mean, 'Okay'? " Bill had turned to face his sister at the same time removing his hand from her arm.

"Look at the will. Mom and Pop get nothing; you and I get everything. You for having Uncle William's name, me for showing him my pussy. Turned out okay."

"Oh Christ. That's no way to look at it."

"Well how else should I?" Then, to put a finality to the whole thing, she said. "Let's go, it's getting late."

"OK." Unable to think of anything more to say and trying to sort through Amy's story; Bill started the car and pulled out onto the highway. At least he now understood why his sister and mother did not get along. Her story also went a long way toward helping to explain why Amy had lived the lifestyle she did; dropping out of college, working for a time in Hooters, then a couple of strip joints, the serial marriages/lovers and now apparently happy to be making a living waiting on tables.

In fact, as he thought further on it he realized he should have suspected something was going on with her. He had, after all, taken a dozen or so seminars and workshops dealing with recognizing child abuse, including the sexual kind. Certainly Amy showed all the signs: overt sexual behavior and dress, alienation from parents and family, multiple sexual partners, and inability to keep a relationship going. Even her glib attitude toward the abuse by their uncle and the living with that Snyder's Corners' guy was not out of character for someone in the state of denial. Mentally he kicked himself before realizing that given she was his sister and the fact he was out of the house when this had happened it was inevitable that he would have missed it. Still, he felt guilty for not knowing and/or doing something about it. He also found himself wondering if there would ever be anything he could do to make it right.

They traveled the rest of the distance to New York City in silence. Bill thought, at one point he heard Amy humming to herself.

"Here you are." Bill said as he pulled up in front of Amy's apartment building.

"Yup, here I are." Amy slid across the seat, planted a kiss on her brother's cheek and retrieved her handbag from the back seat. "Thanks for listening. I hope my expose' didn't upset you too much."

"Let's see, my sister was abused by my uncle, with my mother's permission yet, then spent a summer shacked up with some guy old enough to be her father? Nothing like finding your family closet is full of skeletons to make your day." Bill tried to keep it light and even manage a smile. He did not feel that way.

"Sorry." she got out of the car and started to close the door.

"Hey, Sis!" she stopped door from closing, "About the property and the stuff we inherited. What do you want me to do with it?"

"I don't give a damn. Just get rid of it. If there is any money, we can settle up when you're done." The door closed and she headed across the sidewalk to her apartment building before he could respond.

Suddenly feeling a chill, Bill reached around to the back seat for his jacket. When he pulled it across the seat, the Barbie slid out of the pocket and landed on the passenger seat. Bill, picked it up, stared at it, and then left it on the seat.

Damn, what a day!, he thought as he put the car in gear and drove back to Rye.

— Chapter 8 —

ONE OF THE PRIMARY differences between Tom and Jerry was their approach to the toy train hobby. Tom was a collector, while Jerry was an operator. Like most toy train hobbyists the two fell on a horizontal scale somewhere between two extremes, at one end were the rabid collectors and at the other total layout operators. While neither fit these extremes, they tended to fall somewhere in between these two poles depending on their interests at that particular moment. This position was not stationary but was constantly moving back and forth on the scale as they aged in the hobby and their interests changed, sometimes from one York to another.

At the extreme, the dedicated collector would never place his trains on a piece of track or wire up the accessories, except for display purposes. There are, in fact, many collectors who will not even take the model out of its box but will keep it sealed so it cannot, in any way, get dusty or deteriorate. Some go so far as to x-ray the package to avoid actually opening it at all, they just want to be sure that what they think is in there is, in fact, in there.

Not that all the items collected are new-in-the-box (NIB in the hobby's parlance). Those that are so classified are simply worth more. Most collectibles are used items, many built by defunct companies such as Ives, American Flyer—both absorbed by Lionel—or the original

Marx. Also big in the market are prewar Lionel items built when, by gosh, toy trains were expected to last forever. TCA's bimonthly magazine, *National Headquarters News*, lists classified ads from members offering hundreds of these items for sale or trade; few are new and most are in various states of wear. In fact, TCA has a standards committee whose sole purpose is to define and enforce the grading of these items in relation to their condition. This ten-step standard of classifying toy trains from Mint to Junk is rigid in definition and enforcement. If the buyer and seller disagree on the grade of an item, it is possible to ask members of this committee to arbitrate. Dismissal from the organization can result if a member has too many violations of these standards. There also is a yearly series of <u>Greenberg Pocket Guides</u>, one for each manufacturer, which lists all the products offered by that company over a certain time period. Collectors carry around well-thumbed copies of these guides at train meets and constantly refer to them when buying items.

Collectors cannot abide misrepresentations or counterfeit items since the true originals fetch high prices, which many buyers expect to increase over time. The purchase of trains and train related items by many collectors are investments on which they expect to turn a profit, eventually. At least this was the case until the bottom of the market dropped out in the late nineteen nineties due to the aging and/or dying of many hobbyists, which not only reduced the number of buyers who wanted to obtain the trains of their childhood but also flooded the market with their collected items. Then to erode the market further, some manufactures introduced reproductions that looked exactly like the original, but were more reliable, repairable and operated on modern systems. This allowed many to obtain the model they remember having as a child but to be able to run it using updated transformers and command systems. It also made some manufacturers the enemy for many of the old, hard-line collectors. To their way of thinking, the hobby was going to Hell.

Still there were exceptions. If a particular rare and/or desirable model—like a 1929 Lionel—showed up on eBay or on a table at a meet like, say, York, bidding and prices could sometimes get out of hand. In these cases, it was definitely a seller's market. This was especially true if the item was unused which would make it highly desirable. There were still hobbyists who looked to increase their collections either for their own profit, satisfaction or through the urge to have a complete set of something. Given the right set of circumstances, there were those who were willing and able to pay a lot of money for the right item. Some would even go to illegal means if it meant gaining an edge.

It was common for the modern manufactures to feed the collecting frenzy by offering special run cars and locomotives in particular themes or for hobbyists in select areas. One popular series is a collection of refrigerator cars—reefers to the hobbyist—done using the names and logos of current or defunct breweries. By bringing out these reefers in a continuous series, a manufacturer had a ready-made market for each new item. Along the same lines, soft drink, candy companies and even heavy equipment manufacturers licensed their names and/or logos for placement on the sides of toy reefers, tanker cars and accessories. If this was not enough to suck in buyers, it was common to commemorate events or sport teams by bringing out special models in limited runs either made especially for a select group or offered to the general public. For the hobbyist who bought into this kind of collecting, the expense and space required could be enormous.

While Tom was not at the extreme edge, he took his collecting very seriously, especially in regard to Lionel trains and was determined to obtain the best and rarest. If he were to find a train or accessory that fit his needs, he would fight fiercely for it until he owned it. This was something that carried over from his business ventures and he prided himself on not losing many battles. Since he fairly much had unlimited monetary resources to back him up, he rarely lost if the skirmish came down to money. He would fight to the last dollar to add it to the collection in his basement.

On the opposite end of the scale are the operators. Most of these dedicate their time to running their trains either on their own layouts—some of which can be extensive and expensive—or on the layout of clubs formed with like-minded hobbyists. Generally, these hobbyists are into recently manufactured models, usually those things that fit their particular interest: a railroad line, area of the country or era. In addition, the two major manufacturers, Lionel and MTH, offer different operating systems. While they can be made compatible, they have spawned two opposing camps, and have caused more selectiveness in buying.

Once an operator has purchased the item, be it loco, rolling stock or accessory, they open it, discard the packing material, and place the model on a track or layout to run it. Some of these operators can be very anal, insisting that the models be the exact replica of the prototypes right down to the builder plate location and the number of rivets in the locomotive's boilers. Any deviation from this send them on a rant about the model's manufacturer, which may include contacting the company and/or posting negative comments on the various toy train related forums on the Internet. These pure operators look down their noses at those commemorative items and fancy reefers unless someone can show them an actual photo of the prototype behind a real locomotive.

At their extreme, these operators will do everything they can to make the model look like the genuine article. If the model does not come in the particular road they are interested in, they will repaint and letter it so it does. To make the locomotive and rolling stock look like they would on the real railroad, they will "weather" them, a process by which they cover the model with dirt and grime to make it look used. (Both of these processes horrify collectors who consider them sacrilege.) To the operator these toy trains are to be models of the real thing and they expect to run them that way. Even their layouts closely resemble the real-life settings, some even modeled after actual scenery either from the past using photographs or local landscapes. Most will also make sure to keep maintenance schedules for their locos and rolling stock to keep them in top running condition. There are many in this group of hobbyists who have become quite proficient at repairing and customizing their models and building layouts. Others, if they have the money, hire it done.

Fortunately, most hobbyists fall somewhere between these two extremes. Some run most of their locos but collect certain reefers that they may or may not actually place on the track. Others may have a loco or piece or two of rolling stock displayed in their home or office, but run the rest. Often this particular model has become obsolete so when the hobbyist gets a newer version, he relegates the old one to a shelf because he does not have the heart to stow it away in the closet or attic.

Some hobbyists turn into collectors when they develop an attachment to their toys. Many seem to have collections just because they lack the facilities to lay permanent track but hope to one day—maybe once they retire—build that super layout. Still others run their trains on a seasonal layout—generally Christmas—but keep them packed away for nine or ten months of the year. Often, too, a particular hobbyist changes his position on the collector/operator scale when a windfall comes along or he moves into a new house with room for a layout—or loses one when a baby comes along taking both space and money.

Jerry was the kind of collector who ran most of his trains but was not averse to collecting an item or two if it seemed like a good investment. He managed to come across some commemorative series of reefers that he had sold for considerable profit on eBay or to collectors he met at York. Consequently he was always in the market for a good buy that he did not need to run and would pay well for it if he saw a way to sell it at a profit.

Regardless of where a particular hobbyist fell in the scheme of things, money is spent and most have attics or other storage places filled with discarded packing boxes and idle models. Members of both groups will join the TCA but for different reasons; the collector to buy old things and keep the integrity of the buy/sell part of hobby, the operator to gain access to York to buy the latest thing at blow-out prices. Either way, the two groups share an interest in preserving and expanding their part of the hobby. How to do this is another matter, since neither group can exactly agree on where the hobby is headed or what direction it should take.

It was this difference in outlook that colored what each individual sought when buying items at York.

****

Tom arrived home about ten o'clock on Saturday evening after the five-hour drive from York and dropping Jerry off at his house. It took him only two trips to unload the things he had purchased at the show: two prewar cattle cars, one bascule bridge badly in need of repair, a plastic bag of scenic material that he needed to tweak a part of his layout and some used track. As far as the track was concerned, well, he never seemed to have enough of it most of which he used on the shelves where he displayed his collection.

Aside from one of the cattle cars which was a prewar Lionel model in C-7 condition, (On the ten TCA ten-point condition/grading standards C-7 meant "excellent—all original") and for which he paid four hundred-fifty dollars, he had not seen much of anything that especially interested him. Most of what might have been worth adding to his collection had been in C-4 or lower condition which would have required too much repair work. He had evolved beyond the point where he wanted things that required rebuilding and would only buy things that he could use with what he already was working on. In fact, he had only purchased the bascule bridge so he could cannibalize it for parts to use on another, better one he already owned.

He had hoped his meeting with BoomBoom would turn up something truly unusual, but his New Jersey contact did not have anything for him or a line on anything that he really needed for his collection. Tom had originally gotten to know BoomBoom through eBay, contacted him off-line during a York meet several years ago, and subsequently had purchased some excellent pieces from him. Tom was not sure how BoomBoom came into many of the items, nor did he bother to ask, but the price was always right. If the merchandise came into BoomBoom's hands by less than legal means, it did not bother Tom. Tom had his own secrets as well. Since his collection, being completely privately held, was such that it would never be seen by anyone knowledgeable enough to cause him any problems he did not much care where the items came from, only that they fit his needs.

Tom was glad Becky was already in bed and, not wanting to waken her, pulled out the sleeper bed in his train room and made himself comfortable. Not only had the drive tired him, but the constant arguing with Jerry about the virtues of Lionel over MTH products and the merits or lack thereof of each company's operating systems left him drained. If only Jerry had not been so stubborn to see that Mike Wolf was ruining the hobby with his constant law suits against Lionel, they might have been better friends. As it was, Tom barely tolerated Jerry.

Oh well, tomorrow he would unpack and arrange his purchases where he wanted them. Hopefully, he could forget about VanVierden until the spring York.

As he dozed off, he reminded himself that the next York was only six months off.

****

Jerry had a few more items than Tom. For one thing, he always purchased the MTH commemorative refrigerator car for that particular York meet and picked up their newest catalog. As far as MTH's York reefers were concerned, having the complete set was important to Jerry and this series of cars were the only things that could qualify as collectibles in his train room. He also purchased a new MTH, PRR K-4 locomotive at a blowout price less than two hundred dollars below MSRP from one of the brick and mortar vendors in the main, Orange Hall. (The TCA identified the various exhibition halls on the fair grounds by color: White, Red, Black, Purple, Silver, Blue, Brown and Orange. The Orange Hall—actually the 2003 opened Toyota Arena— was the largest, newest and also held most of the major manufacturers' exhibits.) He now owned both engine numbers in this particular series. Like Tom, he too had purchased some scenic material plus several sets of resin figures that were new to the market. Unlike Tom, Jerry kept to those buildings on the fair grounds where vendors were selling only new items, since he was not interested in that old, used stuff. Instead, he wandered through the manufacturer's displays, especially MTH's, looking for ideas or anything that piqued his interest.

He too was disappointed that BoomBoom had nothing to offer. In the past, after Tom had introduced them, BoomBoom had gotten Jerry some really good buys on new MTH issued items. In fact, his spare DCS remote had come from some of BoomBoom's stock, as did most of his Ross switches and switch motors. Anything Jerry bought was top-of-the-line stuff and he liked the idea of getting it at bargain prices. This time, however, a tapped out BoomBoom had nothing of interest, his explanation being that he needed to restock in time for Christmas. Therefore, like Tom, Jerry made no buys from BoomBoom either.

Jerry was wired from the drive, especially the give and take with Tom, which made him too keyed up to sleep. Also he wanted to check out the new K-4 before turning in. He carefully unpacked it, easing the locomotive out of its package and onto a foam cradle so he could remove the packing from around the wheels and front and rear couplers. He did the same thing with the tender. He then plugged in the tender's tether to the loco, attached it, and carefully placed both on the track at the front of his layout. Using the eyedropper that came with the bottle of smoke fluid, he loaded the smoke unit with several drops of fluid. Next, he dialed up the transformer to twenty volts and programmed the locomotive into his primary DCS handheld. After checking that the loco was in the proper address, he called it up and sent the signal for it to come to life.

There was the prototypical whine of a steam engine starting up, its head light and running lights winked on and, soon, wisps of smoke began to rise from the K-4's stack. Jerry advanced the thumb wheel on the remote and slowly the wheels of the loco began to turn, the chuffs in perfect synchronization with the puffs of smoke rising out of the stack, the drive rods pulling back and forth. Ever so slowly, the K-4 chugged down the track. It gained speed as Jerry thumbed the wheel on the handheld forward, the chuffs rapid firing until they were almost continuous. Taking advantage of the fact that his train room was well soundproofed, Jerry pressed the whistle and the mournful, deep-throated sound came forth, filling the room. For a moment, it transported Jerry back to the days when he watched his father at the throttle of a K-4 pulling out of the freight yard being trailed by a long line of cars. The engineer father always gave a wave and a long blast of the whistle just to thrill the son. Next, Jerry placed his head down close to the track near a curve; this blocked out the rest of the layout and gave him the full effect of a live steam engine headed right at him only to veer away at the last second.

Twice around the loop was enough to assure Jerry that the mechanics and electronics of the product where in good working order. He stopped it, put it into reverse just once to be sure the rear light and reversing unit worked and then shut it down. Tomorrow he would return the model to the cradle and lubricate it before adding it to its permanent place on his railroad.

Fatigue finally caught up with him—it had been a long couple of days, not only wandering around the York Fairgrounds but also helping Tom with the driving. He made sure everything on the layout was powered down, turned off the lights in the train room and went upstairs. Stopping in the kitchen to take his alpha-blocker and supplements and at the bathroom to pee, he finally went in to bed.

As he dropped off, the echo of the K-4 still in his ears, he remembered that it was only six more months to the next York.

****

BoomBoom had a great York. In fact, he came home with his trailer loaded. It took him late into Sunday night to unload and organize the merchandize in his mother's garage.

He started collecting on Tuesday when, while ostensibly helping venders set up in the Holiday Inn's parking lot, he "found" a case of Ross Custom switches that no one seemed to be aware of or to miss. This was a great pickup since these switches are rarely discounted and it meant he could start the bidding just a little under MSRP and they would sell out fast with no questions asked.

On Wednesday, while waiting outside the rear of the Reliance Firehouse, he discovered a Lionel beginner's set and a brand new, in the box, Lionel Polar Express set, left unguarded by the back door. By acting as if he was supposed to be carrying these items into the station, he walked straight through and loaded them in his trailer.

On Friday, after the actual opening of the meet, he did very well working the amateur vendors. At various times he managed to walk out of one hall or the other with a Marklin light tower, an old Ives E Unit, a Lionel prewar flood light tower, and, while haggling with one dealer for some prewar junk, was able to boost a Lionel prewar B & O hopper. He figured this hopper, which was at least a C-6, would bring nearly four hundred dollars, maybe more if bidders went nuts. By the time he had left for his meeting at the Round the Clock Diner, he had had a very successful day.

His big day, however, was Saturday. When the dealers who sold new items were breaking down their booths in the Orange Hall, there was always stuff spread all over the place and, since everyone was tired and anxious to leave, no one was paying too much attention to who was moving what. BoomBoom simply walked around the hall, sometimes helping various dealers carry stuff to their trucks and looking like he belonged. In the meantime, he would take a loco here, accessory there, here a railroad car, there a carton, and hide them under a tarp he had carefully arranged in one out-of-the-way corner. It was no problem for him to be seen with this stuff, since the dealers were used to seeing him walking around with merchandise while helping others.

After most of the dealers in the area where he had hidden his stash had cleared out, BoomBoom simply removed the tarp and acted as if he was tearing down his own booth. Since his trailer had a sign on the side, which read Bergen Trains, everyone who saw him assumed that he was nothing other than a dealer packing up unsold items.

He was always surprised how easily he could get out of the hall with these goods. Often members of the Eastern Division, who were around to help vendors, actually gave him a hand. At one point, one of the workers from one of the dealer booths actually helped by carrying out some the merchandise BoomBoom had ripped off from the guy's employer. The employee never realized the origin of the stuff as he helped BoomBoom load it into his trailer. Among BoomBoom's Saturday haul were the following: three brand new Williams locomotives, half a dozen K-Line passenger car sets, three MTH scale buildings, a whole carton of scenery items, two Lionel starter sets that could be broken up and sold separately, Gargraves track, some more Ross switches and a half carton of MTH York Premier Club membership cars. He had actually carried off this last find from the company's booth. He figured on covering the expenses for his trip with just the locos and the Club cars. The rest would be gravy.

He could not have been happier.

If anything disappointed him, it was that he had not found anything of interest for the two guys from upstate New York. While he had no particular reason to deal with these two, he liked the fact that they paid in cash and were not afraid to part with it for the right item. He was sure, too, that they knew what BoomBoom was up to and that the items were anything but legal, but just did not care. Since they never asked it gave him confidence in dealing with them. They were good customers.

Oh well, BoomBoom thought, *there is only another six months between now and the next York. Maybe I can come up with something by that time.*

****

At the time BoomBoom started to unload his trailer, Bill Weaver was finally able to get to the package sent from Lionel to his uncle. He had gone to the school that morning to retrieve the tests given by his substitute on Friday and spent the better part of the day correcting them. Now, finally finished with this part of his school work, he was sitting at his kitchen table and trying to decide whether he should open the mailing box. Somehow, instinctively, he felt opening it might jeopardize the value. Certainly if, as he suspected, whatever was in the package was a collectible, just opening it might reduce the value. Yet, it was like an itch that needed to be scratched. He placed the package on the table and stared at it. In a way, it mocked him.

Finally, unable to hold off any more, he took the Swiss Army knife he always carried out of his pocket and carefully slit the outer wrapper. Careful not to do any more damage than necessary, he produced just enough opening in the wrapper to slide it off the outer mailing carton. This carton, sealed with a single piece of tape, opened easily and the inner package came out into his hand.

This display box, with Lionel printed on the top and end flaps, was a done in a combination of white, blue and orange with a window in front. Peering inside Bill could see the toy locomotive and tender fastened to a cardboard liner. On closer inspection, Bill could see NY

Central in white lettering on the tender. The locomotive looked real to him.

Turning the box, Bill read "NY Central Hudson, Special Edition, # LN 131928"

Special Edition, Bill thought, that *might mean its worth more than I thought. I'd better check out with John on Monday.*

Still curious but not willing to jeopardize the value of the item further, he slid the package with the locomotive and tender back into the shipping carton and closed the flap. He then placed the carton on the top shelf of the cabinet over the kitchen sink next to the Barbie doll his sister had left in the car and poured himself another cup of coffee. He still had to enter the test scores in his class book before his day was finished.

He had had trouble getting to sleep the night before. The story his sister had told him on their trip back from his uncle's funeral kept jumping to the forefront of his consciousness. It was a nightmare that was only just sinking in. It would be a while before he could think of much else.

— Chapter 9 —

It was a week from Monday before Bill was able to get Amy on the phone. He had tried several times but only succeeded in talking to Givens and Bill did not want to leave a message. What he had to tell his sister dealt with money and he preferred to keep her boyfriend out of it.

"Hi Bro." Amy sounded cheery. "What's up?"

"I've got some information on the toys that we found in the storeroom."

"Good, what do you know?"

"Well, I showed that Barbie and train thing to John Carson—the guy I teach with that's into the action figures. He went nuts about the Barbie."

"Nuts? In what way?"

"Seems that what we have is a Barbie number one. According to what John said, it is a display model that Mattel sent to dealers when Barbie first came out. They are very rare and one in good condition— which this is—could be worth ten grand to the right buyer."

"Wow!"

"Wow is right. Damn good thing you didn't get it when you were ten, you'd have destroyed it."

Amy chuckled. "How about the train thing?"

"John couldn't tell me about that. He said he wasn't up on toy train stuff but, apparently there is a book out there someplace that has prices and stuff in it. He said he'd check around. That's the best he can do. He figures, though, since the box says it is a special edition and, due to the date it was mailed, it may be worth something to somebody."

"Ok, let me know what you find, OK?"

"Will do. Oh, Amy?"

"Yeah?"

"I also told John about the other stuff we left at Snyder's Corners— the other Barbies, Ken dolls and the rest."

"And?"

"He said if it is at all old and in good shape it is worth a lot. Apparently, there is a way to tell the age of the dolls by looking at the patent numbers on their butts. The stuff from back in the early sixties is worth in the five to six hundred dollar range, depending on what condition it is in and how good the packaging is. From the information on that one Barbie and the other stuff I told John about, like the train, it seems a lot of that stuff was stored away and forgotten about long before Uncle William sold the store."

"Maybe he was jerking off so much it rotted his brain so he forgot."

"Sis, you're awful. At any rate it appears there is a windfall, money-wise, there."

"Good, then sell it."

"You're sure."

"Definitely, I don't want any of that shit around. The sooner it's gone the better! I sure as hell don't want it for sentimental reasons." Bill could detect anger rising in her voice.

"Ok. Next question: How do you want to do this? John says there are dealers and liquidators out there who will handle the sale, at a price, for us but the best way is to go through eBay." Although Bill was not an owner of a computer he read enough to have some idea of what eBay was and how, generally, it worked. It just was that there was no way he was going to be able to use it, given his current lack of the necessary computer savvy. "That way you avoid giving up a hellova lot in commissions and, if you get two collectors bidding against each other the price can go sky high. Of course, we can also try and find a collector, privately, and deal one on one with him."

"Do what you want to do. I don't care. Frankly, I don't even care about the money. I'm not rich, but I'm doing ok." For some reason at that moment, Bill had a fleeting memory of his sister silhouetted against the storeroom window. "Just let me know when the whole thing is settled. That includes the building in Snyder's Corners too."

"Yeah, I was going to ask you about that, too. I figure on calling that lawyer, Aaronson, and seeing if he'll handle the renting as he has been while looking for a buyer. That should be the easiest way to go. I sure as hell don't have the time to be running back and forth up there to handle it."

"Whatever works for you on the whole deal is fine with me. I trust you, Bro."

"Thanks for your confidence, that's comforting. As far as the toys are concerned, I think I'll explore the eBay route if I can find someone that can handle it for us."

"That's fine." Then, catching herself, "Oh, do want me to check with Clare? Remember I told you about the gal that works in the diner with me that has a son who sells on eBay? She's always bragging about how well he's doing. Maybe she can give me some tips or even handle it for us."

"Maybe you should do that and get back to me. It would sure save us both time."

"Okay, if I remember, I'll do it when I go into work tomorrow. Anything else?"

"Not that I can think of right now. You take it easy. I love you."

"I will. Talk to you later in the week or early next. Bye." The phone went dead. There was no response to the "I love you".

****

It was six am and Clare Cleary (*I can't help it, I was Clare Johnson until Ian Cleary knocked me up and I hadda marry him.*) was sitting at the end of the Route Seven Diner's counter having her before-work cigarette. *Damn,* she thought, *it is going to be tough when New Jersey's no smoking law kicks in after the first of the year. I'm either gonna hafta quit or find where's else to smoke.* It was not that she was all that addicted but the ritual of a cigarette before work was one she had to follow or her day never went well.

Clare was in her early fifties but looked older. Part of it was a lifetime of work, mostly as a waitress, and the other part was having been a single mother for the last twenty-six years. She had the responsibility of raising her son, Sean, from the time he was two when her husband died. A New York City sanitation worker, Ian was crushed to death by a mobile compactor out at the landfill. Although she had sued the Sanitation Department for wrongful death, the settlement was meager since, as the Department's lawyers argued, successfully, that her husband had been drinking on the job and ignored the compactor operator's warning. This led to his demise. Contributory negligence was the verdict and, after paying her lawyers, the amount of the awarded to Clare barely covered Ian's funeral expenses. Left with a two-year old son and no money, Clare needed a lifetime of dead end jobs to meet expenses. She was now an institution at the Route Seven Diner, having been there for the over twenty-five years.

It was not that Sean had been that hard to raise. Clare was mainly concerned about the usually inner city stuff—drugs, gangs, etc.—that could have tempted him. Fortunately, he seemed immune and, excepting for the damn boom box he was addicted to, he had caused her little trouble. Certainly, she was not happy when he quit high school and loafed around, living at home and mooching meals and money from her but it all turned out ok. He now seemed to be very successful at selling things on eBay. He had his own apartment, a nice car and was constantly on the road buying merchandise. That he had not forgotten his mother and came over for occasional meals helped her realize that she must have done something right in bringing him up. In fact, he was due to come for supper that evening and, despite having a full day of waiting on customers ahead of her, she found herself looking forward to tonight.

Clare checked herself in the mirror at the back of the pie keeper and, straightening her hair net, snubbed her cigarette out and went to her station behind the counter. Just then, Amy, the other waitress on this shift came in.

To Clare, Amy was everything she was not. Young, blue-eyed blonde, with a body that would not stop, and educated to boot, Amy was the focus of attention by most of the male patrons. That was probably why Nick moved Clare behind the counter while Amy served the booths. This meant Amy always seemed to get the biggest tips, which made Clare a bit jealous, something she managed to keep to herself most of the time.

"Good morning, Clare. Another nice day for November, I see."

"Good morning yourself. Seems you're all kinds of chipper today." Clare actually resented the Pollyanna mood of her coworker.

"Just woke up that way, I guess. Sun's out, the starlings are chirping. Guess it's gonna be a nice day." Amy tied her apron around her waist, grabbed an order pad and stuck a pencil behind her ear.

"Sure hope so." Clare was not all that enthusiastic.

****

Things at the diner hit a lull between the early, on their way to work, customers and the old timers who came in for their midmorning coffee. This gave Amy and Clare, the only two servers on duty, some time for a break. Clare took the opportunity to go to the end of the counter, grab a stool and light up. Amy joined her while keeping an eye on the old guy who was finishing up his pie and coffee.

"Can I ask you a couple of questions?" Amy stood behind the counter where she could view the booths.

"I guess so. Whadda bout?"

"Well a couple of weeks ago my brother and I inherited a bunch of stuff from my uncle in upstate New York. Some of it is junk, but there are some toys that my brother says are collectibles. Now, you've told me your son sells stuff on eBay. We're thinking that might be the best place to get rid of these toys and wonder if maybe he could give us some help."

"I don't know but Sean is coming over for supper tonight, I'll ask him. What sorta stuff we talking about? If you don't mind me asking."

"No, I don't mind. It is mostly dolls, Barbies and Kens and some toy trucks and old games. My uncle had a combination hardware and toy store that he closed sometime in the early eighties. The stuff was left in a storeroom since then, just gathering dust as far as I can tell. Most of it is old but never used and is still in boxes that were never opened."

"Sounds like your brother's right, that kind of stuff is collectible. It can be worth real money. I know Sean sells some things like that, mostly toy trains and electronic stuff, but I'll ask."

"Oh yeah, there is one train item. Some old Lionel thing from back in the thirties, I guess. I haven't seen it but my brother has. In fact, my brother has it and a Barbie, all the rest is still up at Snyder's Corners."

"Well I'll talk to Sean tonight and let you know tomorrow."

"Sounds good." At this point Amy's customer raised his coffee cup indicating he needed a refill. She grabbed the coffee carafe and went to help. The conversation was over.

****

Clare had prepared an excellent supper for her son; meatloaf, mashed potatoes and peas, topped off with apple pie. She had not cooked any of it from scratch—in truth she was a terrible cook—but had brought it all home from the diner. She had kept the conversation to chitchat through most of the meal but now, after he had finished off his first piece of pie, she decided it was a good time to pose the topic.

"Sean, you know the girl I work with, Amy?"

"Sure do. That stacked blond with the blue eyes." His mother definitely had BoomBoom's attention. "Why?"

"Now you never mind, she's gotta boy friend and, besides, she's too old for you anyhow." His mother was smiling but she meant the warning. "Apparently she has inherited some old toys from a dead uncle and wanted to know how she could sell 'em on eBay. Seems the guy had a toy store in upstate New York someplace and when he died, she found this stuff stored away."

"Is it really old?" BoomBoom was only vaguely interested. For one thing, unless he could steal the merchandize he did not want to handle it. He saw no sense in adding to his expenses or sharing the profit.

"She said the store closed in the eighties. I guess that would make it 'round twenty-five, thirty years old or older. "

"Well, that stuff'll sell if you can get it into the right category. Tell her that what she needs to do is to log on to eBay, join and then set up a PayPal account. Most bidders like to pay that way and it avoids the hassle of checks and money orders. Then do some looking around in the various categories to see where the stuff you want to sell fits and what kind of prices similar stuff is going for. Once you get to where you want to sell, get some good pictures and post 'em with your ad. It ain't rocket science so if you can follow directions it's pretty easy."

"Could you sell it?"

"Nope. I ain't interested in jobbing for someone else. I've enough stuff to handle without that kinda hassle."

"Ok, I'll tell her. I'm sure she'll appreciate it. More pie?"

BoomBoom, who always liked Nick's pie, helped himself to another wedge. "Any toy trains in that batch of toys?"

"I think she said there was one. Lionel, I think she said." Clare stopped to think. "Yeah, something from back in the thirties."

"Thirties?" Now BoomBoom was a little interested. "Are you sure?"

Clare thought again, trying to remember the conversation with Amy. "Yea, I'm sure she said the thirties."

"Now that is something I might be interested in." BoomBoom put down his fork. "Would you ask her if it has a model number and, if so, what it is?"

"If I remember, Dear." Clare smiled as she put a third piece of pie on her son's plate

"Thanks, Ma, I gotta couple of weeks' worth of shows and stuff, so if she's willing to talk about it, I'll get back to you as soon as I can.

****

It was not until they were on a break on Thursday that Clare remembered to tell Amy, as best she could remember, how to get started selling on eBay. She also told Amy that, while Sean could not sell things for them on eBay, he was interested in the train's model number. Amy carefully wrote everything down that Clare shared with her so she could report it to Bill. Also, at Clare's repeated behest, she even wrote herself a second reminder to ask Bill for the model number on the Lionel train thing.

She called Bill that night after work and passed the information on. He thanked her and gave her the Lionel catalog number. She wrote it down and gave it to Clare the next day. It happened that BoomBoom stopped by his mother's the following Sunday evening to retrieve some items from her garage so she gave him the slip of paper that Amy had given her.

Once BoomBoom had finished packing his weekend eBay sales for shipment, he fished the note his mother gave him out of his pocket, unfolded it and noted the number. It was nothing he had seen before, so he got down his copy of <u>Greenberg's Pocket Guide to Lionel Trains, 1901 – 2004</u> to look the number up. When he saw the result, he leaped out of his chair and dug through a pile of papers on his desk until he found Tom Bisignani's phone number and called it.

— Chapter 10 —

TOM WAS NOT EXACTLY excited when BoomBoom called. He had been in the midst of making a deal for shipping two hundred pallets of stone fence rock to a dealer in Hawaii the first week in March and was not quite sure where the fieldstone was coming from. Since winter was about to close in on Palatine County, digging out stone was not going to be easy, especially if there was the usual amount of snow. He found himself hoping against hope, for either a mild winter or a February thaw to facilitate the collection. Otherwise, his contractors and their stackers were going to be hard pressed to meet the order. In this context, he was not especially eager to hear about a possible rare locomotive and tender that Cleary had found. He wrote down the information and put it aside.

It was not until later in the evening that he was able to put aside his worries, retrieve the Lionel ID and other information from BoomBoom that he had jotted down and do some checking on it. First checking in his copy of Greenberg, he was able to find only basic information about this particular locomotive. Specifically, that it was an uncataloged one which meant there would not be any information about the set in any of the old Lionel catalogs in Tom's collection. The fact that this locomotive was from 1929 and produced in limited quantities intrigued him. This sent him elsewhere for information on the item and its value.

Tom had amassed, over the twenty years of train collecting, almost as many books and magazines about trains as he had models of them. This collection consisted of magazines that he carefully classified by publication and year, manufacturer's catalogs—primarily Lionel—and a few dozen books on collectible trains and their accessories. This library took up most of a large, back storage area adjacent to his train room and was probably worth in excess of ten thousand dollars. Knowing this particular Lionel issue was uncataloged meant Tom could disregard the catalogs and concentrate on the magazines and books. As luck would have it, a search of his collection of TCA's *The Train Collectors Quarterly* turned up an article in the April 1989 edition written on the sixtieth anniversary of the locomotive's release.

According to the article, Lionel made only fifty of these pairs and gave them out as dealer appreciation sets in the summer and fall of 1929. By 1989, the whereabouts of only three was known—two were in public displays and one in a private collection in Canada. The rest, presumably, had been sold or given to customers and were tucked away in attics or resided in the bottom of landfills. Unfortunately, at the time and due to Lionel having changed its corporate location and reorganized a number of times, any record of the dealer recipients of the Hudson and its tender was lost, making tracking them down almost impossible. A search made by the article's author of the few big Lionel dealerships in operation in the 1930s and still in business in 1989, turned up no leads. The author assumed that, if found, one of these locomotives in a reasonably good condition would be worth five or six thousand dollars. He did not hold out much hope for anyone finding such a deal. Included with the article were several black and white photographs of one of the originals from Lionel's archives.

Five or six thousand dollars!! Tom thought, *that's in 1989 dollars. I bet that set, if BoomBoom is right, will be worth over twice as much.*

Putting down the article, Tom found he was now excited about the prospect of being able to own such a collectible. It would be the crowning achievement to his train collecting if he could pull it off.

He immediately tried to call BoomBoom but, for whatever, reason no one answered. (Tom had no way of knowing that, at that moment, BoomBoom was off on a restocking job of his own.) Disappointed, Tom needed someone to share this news with and, knowing that Becky would not be interested, thought of Jerry.

It was not that Jerry and Tom were that close, but aside from himself, there was no one in Palatine County to share this news with. Other than their interest in the toy train hobby, membership in TCA, and sharing a ride to the semiannual York train meet, the two men had little in common. Although Tom undoubtedly sold rock and bluestone to the contractors that Jerry worked with in Westchester County, they had never met until Jerry discovered Tom's name in TCA's *Directory of Information* and called him. If the truth were known, Tom really did not much care for Jerry on several levels. First was that Jerry was not a native Palatinate but rather had moved in from downstate and seemed to be one of those liberal, downstate, Democrats. Second, as a hobbyist, Jerry was more interested in running his trains than collecting them. Finally, and more damning, Jerry was a MTH Moonie. This persuasion added to the above created a schism that, as far as Tom was concerned, could never be bridged.

****

Aside from the collector/operator division in the toy train hobby, there was another, often extreme, division of loyalty: Lionel vs. MTH. The former enthusiasts, known as Louies, only purchased from and were entirely faithful to, Lionel. As such, they were willing to fight to the death anyone who cast any dispersion on this company. While there were a few other companies that built locomotives and rail cars, it was MTH that drew their greatest ire. They regarded MTH as an upstart company who had stolen most of what was good from Lionel and repackaged it as its own product. That MTH had sued Lionel for stealing preproduction designs through its Korean manufacturer and won the suit for millions in damages only inflamed them to a greater degree. This made Mike Wolf and his companies the Evil Empire as far as the extremist Louie's were concerned. They insisted on dating anything and everything wrong with the hobby back to MTH's first train offering in 1996. Finally, they insisted that MTH's digital operating system would fail prior to its introduction and when it proved otherwise, pounced on every glitch and flaw even as MTH's engineers succeeded in correcting them.

The MTH loyalists or Moonies (Not to be confused with members of Sun Myung Moon's Unification Church, this was the designation given to MTH supporters by a blogging wag who needed a name beginning with "M" to distinguish this group.) on the other hand could not help but poke fun at Lionel for being an antiquated company with outdated products—while never acknowledging that MTH had problems. Moonies insisted on repeating variations on the story that, at one point, Wolf was a loyal Lionel dealer who had been disenfranchised by Lionel's CEO because Mike had ideas the CEO did not like. Consequently MTH was the proof that Lionel was on its way down. The Moonies touted Mike—they always referred to him by his first name—as an innovator whose company was the future of toy trains. As proof, they offered MTH's digital operating system as being the one that would eventually control the market since it was compatible with Lionel's system and upgradeable while Lionel's lacked innovation, was behind the times, and would not work with MTH's. In addition, the fact that MTH won the law suit, which may or may not have forced Lionel to declare bankruptcy, gave the Moonies even more salt to rub into the Louies' wounds and kept the pot boiling. To the Moonies' way of thinking, Lionel cheated and rather than own up to it and pay the judgment, they ducked it by seeking bankruptcy protection. They loved to bring this up at every opportunity.

While the majority of the hobbyists ignored this controversy and just bought the trains and accessories they liked regardless of who made them, the lunatic fringe at the opposite ends of this dichotomy kept the controversy in a constant uproar. Often, hobbyists on the sidelines went so far as to give a little nudge to either side just to watch the sparks fly.

This was Jerry's position. Rather than being a full-fledged Moonie; he often gave the needle to Tom just to see what reaction he could elicit. Since Jerry felt Tom was a pompous ass about the whole thing, he rather enjoyed seeing the reaction. Tom, on the other hand, who had the genetic predisposition for the lack of a sense of humor, was a serious Louie who failed to see anything amusing in the situation and did not much care for this needling.

****

Therefore, it was not out of companionship that Tom put aside for the moment his aversion and called Jerry to tell him about the Lionel train. It was just because Tom was so excited about the information about such a rare find that he needed to share the news with someone he hoped would understand.

Jerry, to some extent, did.

Now Jerry was not a collector per se and Lionel stuff, as a rule, did not interest him. However, Jerry was interested in investing and, if what Tom told him was true then this train, even for a Lionel, sounded like a hell of an investment. Without tipping his hand, Jerry pumped Tom for as much information as he could about the train and began running some numbers in his head. In short order, he figured if he could buy the set for, say, in the neighborhood of ten grand and turn around and sell it for twelve at the next York, it would earn him a tidy profit. Then too, there was the competition factor of beating Tom out of the deal. If the truth be known, Jerry resented Tom's "holier than thou" attitude toward MTH in general and Jerry in particular and just outdoing Tom on this deal would give Jerry a great deal of satisfaction. To Jerry's way of thinking, Tom was a Republican, Louie, pompous ass that needed to be brought down a peg or two. In fact, the more he thought about it, the more Jerry decided he would go all-in on this deal, profit be damned. He had to one-up Tom without concern to cost. The first thing he would have to do was contact BoomBoom to cut a deal.

As soon as Tom hung up, Jerry dialed BoomBoom's number. He had no better luck than Tom had had earlier.

****

By the middle of the following week, BoomBoom knew he was on to something that was going to be very profitable. Both Jerry and Tom had contacted him about the waitress' train. Tom had told BoomBoom that he would be willing to pay five thousand dollars for the set with ten percent going to BoomBoom as a finder's fee. BoomBoom got the impression this was only an opening offer. Jerry did not mention a dollar amount but the inkling BoomBoom got from the conversation was that he would at least match any amount Tom was willing to offer while giving BoomBoom a bigger cut. Now all BoomBoom had to do was get his hands on the set. To this end, he sent word by way of his mother, that he wanted to meet with Amy. Ostensibly this meeting was to give her further details about eBay but his real reason was to, somehow, get her to sell him the train or at least handle the sale for her.

There was a slight time problem, however. For one reason or another, mostly because this time of year was big for electronics and train shows which kept BoomBoom busy, the meeting never took place until the week before Christmas. It was set for the Route Seven Diner and, through his mother's advice, at a midmorning time when Amy would not be too busy. BoomBoom came at ten.

"Damn, its cold out there." BoomBoom smiled at his mother and shook some of the gray/white snow off his jacket. The temperatures were in the low thirties but with the humidity and wind, it felt colder. Amy, seeing him come in and figuring out he must be Clare's son came up front as BoomBoom was hanging his coat on the edge of a booth. She smiled as she approached him.

"I'm BoomBoom...er Sean" He was not sure what name his mother had used so he covered both bases.

"Which is it? Sean or BoomBoom?" Even Amy's waitress outfit did not hide her body—something that contributed to her tips—and she felt the young man giving her a once over.

"Ma calls me Sean, but my friends call me BoomBoom." *Damn*, he thought, *she sure looks fine!* "Why don't you call me BoomBoom?" He took a seat at the counter.

"Ok BoomBoom what's the story on the eBay?" She did not sit, but leaned over with her hands on the counter. In this position, BoomBoom was just able to get just a glimpse of her bra covered breasts over top of the scoop neck of her waitress uniform. She intended for this to happen.

"Basically it's really easy to do." For a second, overwhelmed by the view, he almost forgot what he was going to say. Collecting himself, he thought back and then just repeated most of what he had told his mother. "Just set up two accounts, one with eBay and one with PayPal. The PayPal account will allow you to have your seller deposit payment right into your account; you won't hafta mess around with checks and stuff. Then, take a good picture of the item and post it in the right category—or a couple of 'em—set a starting price and wait. Pretty soon, you'll be getting bids on the stuff. Once the auction is over, mail the stuff to the winner. Oh yeah, make sure you ask enough for postage so you don't get hosed on that." Since he was more interested in the train set, he had to make sure he did not trip his hand by appearing too eager.

"That's pretty much what Clare told me. Is that's all there is to it?"

"Yup. The important thing is to make sure you've got a good picture up so they know what they're buying and its condition. And to make sure it is in the right category—otherwise it'll get missed."

"You mean like toys?" Amy was not certain how she could classify what they had to sell.

"I'd go a bit deeper than that. Toys might be a bit too general. What is it you're trying to sell?"

"I think I told your mother. Mostly Barbie and Ken dolls from the sixties. Some toy trucks and a train set."

"Well, the Barbie and Kens have their own category. As far as the trucks are concerned, if they're real old you might want to double advertise them as toy trucks and collectibles." And now he had his opening. "As for the train, there are specific categories for each gauge and manufacturer."

"Gauge?"

"Yeah, the toy trains come in different gauges, depends on the size track they use. If I remember, Ma said yours is an old Lionel. That probably means O gauge. If you have it here, I could check if for you. I sell a lot of that stuff."

"Oh no, none of the stuff is here. Some, like the train, is at my brother's over in Rye. We left the rest up at the storage place in Snyder's Corners."

Snyder's Corners? No, it couldn't be. This stuff came from the same place as those two old guys live? Even BoomBoom understood the irony of that.

"Only one problem," Amy brought BoomBoom out of his thoughts. "neither my brother nor I have a computer."

Great, though BoomBoom, *this is perfect. Now all I need is to get her to let me handle it.*

"Tell you what." He finally offered after a pause, trying not of appear too anxious or excited. "I gotta deal for you. Since you only have the one train to sell, why mess around with it on eBay and postage and stuff? I handle a lot of that kind of thing, I can even find a deal with collectors off line. Why don't you bring it in and let me have a look at it? If it's worth anything I'll either pay you for it or help you sell it; your choice."

"That sounds like an idea. Want to handle the rest of the stuff too?"

"Not really. I'm not in to toy stuff, just trains and electronic gear. 'Sides the toys shouldn't be hard to get rid of this time of year. People will be falling all over theirselves to get it."

"Well, let me talk to my brother and I'll get back to you. Should I just go through your mother?"

"You don't need to. Here's my cell number." BoomBoom slid his business card—he made them several hundred at a time on his PC—

across the counter to her. Then since their business seemed to be over and he did not want to leave, "How's about a piece of apple pie and a cuppa coffee?"

"Sure. Coming right up." Amy turned to go to the coffee urn. BoomBoom now was able to focus on her ass as she walked away.

****

It took two days before Amy managed to get hold of Bill. By that time and at the urging of John, Bill had done some research on the Lionel set. Because of what he found, the price was going to go up.

— Chapter 11 —

ONCE JOHN CARSON FOUND LN 131928 was a limited edition, he encouraged Bill to do some real checking to see what it was worth. Since John was not familiar with collectible trains, he suggested Bill go to some hobby shop that sold new items to learn more about its value. Bill took the advice and that weekend went into Rye Hobbies and Trains.

The owner, while admitting that he was not up on collectibles, was helpful by steering Bill to one of his customers who was a member of the Train Collectors Association. This customer, who was primarily an operator and belonged to TCA only as a means of gaining entry to the York meet, gave Bill the phone number of the Toy Train Reference Library in Strasburg, Pennsylvania. The secretary at the library gave Bill the name of Bill Farmer a TCA member who volunteered in the library and who, she assured him, was knowledgeable about collectibles and would be more than happy to lend a hand.

He made arrangements to call Farmer when he was working at the museum.

Farmer was especially excited after Bill gave him the mailing date and the item number of the Lionel set because he recognized that the locomotive would have to be old and rare. Farmer went directly to the

TCA's Library and, searching the archives, turned up the same article in the *1989 Train Collectors Quarterly* that Tom Bisignani had found in his collection several weeks earlier. Once Farmer had this information about the history of the item and its rarity, he was able to give Bill a better indication of its value.

"As far as I can tell, it hasn't even been out of the box." Bill offered.

"That would make sense. Considering it was made just as the Depression was starting. A toy train like that, especially one in the two hundred dollar plus range, was probably hard to sell in late '29."

"That's kind of what I figured. Must be my uncle stuck it away and then forgot about it."

"Well, I'd give you the five grand for it right now, if I had it." Farmer offered "But if you shop it around, I'm sure you could easily get twice that. After all, it is the probably only one of four in existence and if, from what you say, it hasn't been run, it would be much more valuable to some collector."

"That much?" Bill queried. "For a toy?" It was more than Bill had dreamed it would be worth.

"Oh yeah." Farmer chuckled, "To some collectors, these aren't toys; they're either investments or pieces of a collection that has gotten out of hand. If, as you say it's hasn't been run then it'll be worth a lot more. Put it on eBay and collectors will be stumbling all over themselves to buy it."

"Well eBay isn't a possibility for me. I don't own a computer. Any other way I could sell it?"

"Well, there are a lot of people out there that, for a commission, would sell it for you either on eBay or directly to collectors. If you want, I can put you in touch with someone that may be able to locate a buyer for you."

"If that's the only other way then I'll have to pass. My sister has already found someone who says he can broker a deal for us." Bill hunted through the business cards he had pinned to the bulletin board over his desk looking for BoomBoom's card that Amy had sent to him. "OK, here it is, BoomBoom Cleary."

"Never heard of him but that doesn't mean he's not good. Is he a member of TCA?"

"Let's see. Oh yeah, it says here that he's member of TCA. There's a seven digit number at the bottom of the card, too."

"That would be his membership number, give it to me and I'll check the TCA's *Directory of Information* to see what his membership status is."

Bill read the number to Farmer over the phone. There was a period of silence on the other end and Bill could hear papers rustling

The *Directory of Information* is broken into three sections, all of which are a complete listing of active TCA members: one is in numerical order by membership number, the first two digits of which were the year the person joined; the second is an alphabetical list by member names; in the third members are grouped by state and city of residence. Farmer went first to the numeric listing to check to see what name belonged to the membership number Bill had given him, he then he cross-referenced the name in the alphabetical listing. This listing was the most comprehensive, giving out whatever information the member wanted shared: address, phone number, email address, and TCA division being the most common. Further the member could also list whether he had an operating layout, wanted visitors to stop in and see it, and the type/brand of trains he preferred. Armed with this information, Farmer got back on the phone with Bill.

"Yup, he a member alright, he's not listed as BoomBoom though, but Sean Cleary. There is no preference to what kinds of trains he prefers listed though. Just an address, phone number and email address. Want them?"

"I've got his business card with his phone number on it and that should be enough, thanks. Do you figure he's legit?"

"I don't have anything listed against him. I see from his membership number that he's been in TCA for about four years so if he were up to no good, we'd heard about that by now. Normally you can figure if he's a TCA member somebody's recommended him so he's probably ok."

"Then I should deal with him?"

"I don't see why not. But if you think he's lowballing you on price, contact me again and I'll give you the names of a couple other members that may help."

"Ok, I'll do that."

"Good luck. You've got yourself a valuable collectible there. I hope you're successful selling it. Good bye."

"I hope so too. Thanks for your help. So long." Bill hung up, picked up the package containing the loco and tender with a new appreciation for its value.

Up to this point, it was just another toy that he wanted to get rid of. Now, finding out how much it was worth had changed his prospective. He started to treat it with more care, worrying that he might do something to it that somehow would diminish its value. As a result, he would no longer place it on the high shelf in the kitchen, too much danger of it falling and becoming damaged. From this point on Bill would keep the train in its mailing carton under his bed.

He immediately called Amy and, not being able to catch her home, left a message with John Givens for her to call him back. He wanted her to set up a meeting with Cleary.

****

Tom Bisignani was beginning to be concerned about the Lionel train deal he had with BoomBoom. Christmas and New Years had come and gone, the weather was lousy and the set was still not in his hands. In addition, BoomBoom had dropped a couple of hints to the effect that the owner of the set wanted more money and that there was, possibly, another person bidding on it. Neither made Tom very happy.

For one thing, Tom was used to making deals quickly. In his business dealings, he found that as soon as he and his buyer agreed on Tom's price, that was the best time to close the deal before common sense or another deal prevailed. In Tom's experience, the longer a deal remained open, the more likely it was that it would unravel. In the case of this model, that seemed to be happening. Tom was determined to own this item, even if he had to overpay for it, and so far this inability to firm up a price bothered him. Now there was this hedging and Tom was beginning to wonder if BoomBoom was not screwing him over. If there was one thing Tom Bisignani did not like, it was someone trying to screw him over.

Just to keep the pressure on, Tom made it a priority to call BoomBoom at least once every other day or so. Since he had BoomBoom's cell phone number it made it possible to get him wherever and whenever he felt the need. Tom was hoping this constant nagging somehow would irritate BoomBoom enough to get him off his butt and force a deal. Thus far, it was not working.

****

Oh, BoomBoom was getting pissed all right, but there was not that much he could do to move the deal along. For one thing, he was ignoring his one cardinal rule about not getting greedy. Seeing how much both of these guys wanted that model and sensing they would pay top dollar for it, BoomBoom was loathe to do the deal without both men in on the action. This was what was responsible for the delay.

To make matters worse, Jerry VanVierden and his wife had left for San Juan just before Christmas. While BoomBoom was still able to contact Jerry via phone, not having Jerry physically in the area meant BoomBoom could not pin him down on a deal. For one thing, Jerry wanted to see the merchandise before making a concrete commitment to buy it and, since he left before BoomBoom, himself, had actually seen the locomotive, this was not possible. Consequently, BoomBoom could not give Jerry an honest appraisal of the condition of the train.

Therefore, BoomBoom hedged and hawed and, in the meantime, the seller was getting more information, which was bound to drive the price higher. In one respect, this did not especially bother BoomBoom as he figured the higher the price went, the higher his finder's fee would go. The last time BoomBoom talked to VanVierden, Jerry had told BoomBoom that he and Katrina would be coming back to Snyder's Corners in early February. This was earlier than they normally came back, but it seemed Katrina had some sort of organizational meeting for her golf league scheduled during that month.

At about the same time Jerry confirmed he was returning, BoomBoom finally, after being held up by his Christmas rush and Bill's preparing his students for midyear exams, was able to have his first face-to-face meeting with Weaver. Now, at last, he would get to see LN131928 for the first time.

****

The meeting took place at the Route Seven Diner on the third Saturday in January. Bill had the Lionel Hudson with him. They took a booth in the back of the diner where, after Amy brought BoomBoom the usual piece of pie and coffee, she joined them. Bill, who had arrived first, only had a coffee. Since he did not want to seem overanxious, BoomBoom waited until he had finished his pie before asking to see the locomotive. Carefully, more mindful now of its value, Bill slid the cardboard carton out of the shipping box and held it where BoomBoom could see it.

"I won't let you take it out of that box." Bill said as a way of explanation for not handing the package over to BoomBoom. He turned the package so BoomBoom could see the locomotive and tender through the cut-out window. "Maybe if you find someone that is interested in buying it then he could actually take it out."

"That's probably a good idea. The people who collect these things want 'em in as immaculate a form as possible." BoomBoom could see the loco was in pristine shape. While he was not a collector or really interested in trains, he had seen enough of them to know a good one when it was in front of him. This was a good one.

"How are you coming on a buyer?" Bill left the package on the table but did not offer to hand it to BoomBoom or move it any closer. *He's seen enough to know what it is, let it go at that.*

BoomBoom motioned for Bill and Amy to bring their heads closer to his. In a conspiratorial low voice, he said, "I got two of them interested. Both in upstate New York."

"Two?" Bill was as happy as he was surprised. "Where in upstate New York?"

"Sorry, pal, can't tell you." BoomBoom smiled. "You might figure on cutting out the middleman and going to them directly." Now that BoomBoom had his hooks into this train he was not about to give either Bill or Amy a chance to double-cross him and cut him out of the deal.

"Now why would we do that?" It was Amy who was more than a bit incredulous.

"Understand, it's not that I don't trust you, it's just that in my business I've learned to be careful." BoomBoom was still smiling. Then, more to impress Amy, he said, "Don't worry, these guys are rich SOB's that'll pay plenty to own this, maybe ten, twelve grand. I figure on getting them to bid against each other to drive up the price."

"OK, let's talk price." Bill wanted to get down to particulars. "How much of the selling price are you gonna want?"

"Fifteen percent would be about right."

"We'll give you ten." It was Amy who sensed that the fifteen was just BoomBoom's starting point. She also was aware that BoomBoom was coming on to her and figured she could use this to lower his commission.

"Twelve and a half." BoomBoom looked from Amy to Bill and back to Amy.

"Nope, Ten." Amy was as adamant as she was sure she had the right number.

A pause, then, reluctantly so as not to give anything away, "OK, ten it is. You're killing my profit on this though." Of course, this was gravy for BoomBoom anyway since either Jerry or Tom was going to pay him a finder's fee, probably another ten percent, on the other end. Regardless of who bought the trains and how much they paid, BoomBoom was going to be a big winner. Besides, given his lack of math skills, he probably would have had trouble figuring out a twelve and a half percent commission any way.

"Agreed." Bill reached across the table and stuck out his hand.

"Agreed." BoomBoom took the hand offered. "Well, I gotta go. I'll be in touch." He pushed back from the table and stood. "Oh yeah, one other thing."

"And that would be?" Bill asked as he slid the locomotive and tender back into the mailing box.

"Both of these guys will probably want to see the merchandise before they pay for it. You wouldn't mind taking a ride upstate would you?" BoomBoom looked back and forth from Amy to Bill.

"Not at all. But I teach school during the week so it would have to either be on a weekend or during our Presidents Week vacation that starts on the fifteenth of February." Bill had answered for both.

"I'll see what I can do." BoomBoom pulled his coat on and headed for the door. Reaching it, he stopped, turned back, and smiled. It was meant for Amy.

****

Jerry arrived back at the house in Snyder's Corners early on the evening of the second of February. As soon as he got everything in the house back into operation, he called BoomBoom and asked him if he could do something about setting up a meeting with the owners of the Lionel set. BoomBoom said he would try to get it set up for the school's Presidents Week vacation.

BoomBoom then put in a call to Bill Weaver to see what days would be the best time to set up the meetings with his buyers. Bill told him anytime the week of the fifteenth but, if he was going to have to travel to upstate New York, he wanted to be sure that the weather was going to be good. BoomBoom agreed since being snowbound in some hick town by lousy weather was not his idea of anything he wanted to do either, even if this meant having to spend time with Bill's sister.

Finally, BoomBoom was able to give Tom Bisignani a call before Tom could call him. With a firm date, he was able to alert Tom that the meeting was going to come off sometime during that week of February. Tom was happy to hear this but it created some anxiety as well. The load of stone bound for Hawaii was supposed to be coming into the dock that week and he wanted to be there to make sure of a correct count. If that was the case and he was in the dock, the meeting would have to take place there.

BoomBoom said that he would see what he could do and would get back to everyone as soon as he was assured the weather would cooperate.

****

Happily, for everyone involved, the weather looked like it was going to be excellent for President's Week. A low was stagnating right over the upper Ohio Valley and it was pumping warm weather up from the southwest, pushing in unusual sunny, sixty-degree weather. This not only would assure that traveling in and out of Palatine County would be uncomplicated, but it meant the rock pickers would be able to do get on with the job of filling the pallets for shipping to Hawaii.

The geographic location of the Catskill Plateau is such that any one of three weather patterns can influence its weather. Although they are year around weather systems, in the winter all have the capability of producing cold weather and a lot of precipitation—usually snow—or warm weather with a lot of sun. To make matters worse, sometimes these systems can hit the area in rapid succession. At other times, they seem to disappear all together. Couple these systems with the effect the crisscross of valleys and nooks and crannies of the topology can have on wind movement, forecasting the weather for the area can be a very uncertain vocation making the use of computer generated weather models akin to using an Ouija board. It also means the inhabitants of the area have to be ready for almost anything.

The most common of the cold weather patterns arises as the result of the prevailing westerly or northwesterly winds. These winds pick up air masses in the Arctic; move them over Canada through Northern Minnesota or Michigan, then over the open waters of the Great Lakes of Erie and/or Ontario where the air picks up moisture. Once ashore, this air rises, cools further, and the moisture condenses into droplets. When the droplets become heavy enough, they fall as rain, sleet or snow, depending on the season and temperature. This "Lake Effect" precipitation can be as minor as snow showers or "streamers" that fall in one area, while the neighborhood right next door is in sunshine. Then there are the snow squalls, which can produce low wind chills, whiteouts, two or three inches of snow very quickly and then stop. On the other hand, the "Lake Effect Machine" can produce major amounts of snowfall over wide areas when the pattern persists for a week or longer, dumping a total of up to a foot or better—sometimes at an inch or so per day, at others three inches in an hour. In addition, and depending on the force of the wind and the temperatures, this snowfall can occur close in to the lakes or miss them and pop up miles inland. While this system primarily reaches the western slopes of the Catskills, when the winds are howling, it can make it as far east as the Hudson Valley. Usually, however, the deeper snows occur further north than Palatine County and this system just brings in cold air. All of this cold weather, especially if it occurs early in the season before there is a great depth of snow will cause the ground to freeze rapidly and to great depth.

The second system, and maybe the worst when it produces snow and cold, is the Nor'easter. This condition occurs when a low-pressure system forms over the Atlantic, stops just offshore of New England, and pumps moist air off the ocean that collides with cold Canadian air. Under the right circumstances, it may affect the whole of the Catskills. Depending on how far offshore the low parks itself and the placement of the cold air; this system can produce a good, old-fashioned blizzard. While the amount of snow can be prodigious, especially if the ground is frozen, it is the temperatures falling below zero, and low wind chills that make these storms so nasty. In the grips of a Nor'easter, the area can become extremely inhospitable. Fortunately, a real Nor'easter rarely hits the area more than once a season and, even then, misses most parts of the Catskills, settling on the eastern or northern slopes.

When the snow is around, it has an advantage of hiding the junk piles and old cars that are signs of civilization and making one forget for a time that they are there. As soon as there is a midwinter thaw, they will resurface as a reminder of man's planned obsolescence. When this happens, the ground, which was frozen rock solid by earlier systems to better allow the snow to accumulate on it, will be impenetrable by the runoff of the snowmelt until the frost is driven out of it. This snow water is important, however, since it feeds the five rivers that drain the mountains and will quench the thirst of the citizens of New York City. Dams in the Schoharie, two branches of the Delaware, Neversink and Esopus create reservoirs, which collect this runoff and feed it through underground conduits to the City. Only the Susquehanna leaves the mountains unfettered.

Palatine County is located in such a way that it takes the brunt of these systems. This give credence to the citizen's saying, "If you don't like the weather wait a minute, it'll get worse." Depending on the system and the county, the Catskills can be a cold, gloomy place with a lot of snow and little sunshine one minute and sunny, balmy and snow free the next.

As luck would have it Palatine County had experienced both of the storm systems during December and January and there was a lot of snow on top of frozen ground. Now the weather was to turn to the third system, the warm one.

This warm weather occurs when the jet stream makes a dip in such a way that the winds come up out of the southwest because the steering low stagnates someplace in the Midwest. This brings air in from as far away as the Gulf of Mexico. Overriding the southern states, the air is warm, often moisture laden, and slides up the Appalachian chain in the Carolinas, Virginia, Tennessee, or Pennsylvania. It then overrides the Pocono's and slams into the southwestern edge of the Catskills. How much precipitation the area receives depends on the path the storm takes, the temperatures, and how fast it is moving. If the jet stream's path stagnates right on top of the mountain chain, the system will first drop a lot of rain in a short period of time and then dry up. If the temperatures are not extreme, much of the precipitation falls in the northern most area as sleet or, worse still, freezing rain, which causes more problems for the inhabitants. For the most part, this kind of a system does not produce extremely low temperatures and, often, as the air rises it dries and warms becoming almost benign, so instead of winter weather conditions, it brings a taste of spring in the midst of this winter season. When this happens, especially if it persists for a week or longer, the snow that had accumulated melts, some green shoots may appear, and residents come out of their houses to pursue springtime activities. This is only a respite from winter, as soon as the whole system gets moving again it will be replaced by the vengeful return of cold and snow.

There is another aspect to this warm weather, however. Until the frost leaves the ground in late spring, this midwinter thaw's water trickles over the frozen earth and mixes with mountain's brick red soil. Unable to penetrate the frozen ground, this combination of earth and water creates what the locals' call the mud season where this mixture covers everything from the sides of vehicles to the boots of men that have to work in it. Eventually, however, the watery mud, along with pieces of rock, flow into the feeder streams, coloring them, and, moving on; eventually reaching the reservoirs where it settles to the bottom. Therefore, every winter and spring and ever so slowly, the streams are filling the reservoirs with silt and destroying their ability to hold water. Man is facilitating this by his removal of vegetation through lumbering, loosening of the soil by farming and bringing soil to the surface when quarrying. Ultimately, through the work of Mother Nature and with a big dose of help from humans, this silting will render the Catskills reservoirs useless. This is especially bad when the thaw is preceded by one of those southwestern rain/sleet storms

Winter's snow and frost only hasten this process and in those years where there are several unexpected thaws, the process is accelerated. This spring happened to be one of those years.

— Chapter 12 —

THE WARM WEATHER WAS proving a mixed blessing for Peter Potts. While the lack of snow made it easier to locate and dig out stone, the thawing of the upper layer of ground over the lower, still frozen solid, layer made it tough to maneuver either of his Bobcats. Whether trying to move a pallet of rock or dig up boulders sticking above ground, the Bobcats slipped and slid. At one point, one of the Bobcats hit a slick spot and threatened to slide sideways down a hill. This near accident cost Peter a loaded pallet. Another time he spent the better part of two hours rocking back and forth to get the other loader free of an especially deep quagmire. *Well,* he thought, *at least it's warm and isn't raining any more.*

Up until three years ago, Peter had been trying to make a living as a dairy farmer on sixty acres of hardscrabble farm at the edge of Ferrioville. He was severely disadvantaged in this pursuit. His first problem was that he had not inherited his farm but though some misguided notion, had tried, after graduating from the high school in Snyder's Corners with a major in agriculture, to start farming from scratch. This notion was that farming was for the independent minded outdoor lover had proved not to be enough to keep the bank and the tax collector from his doorstep. After plunging into considerable debt, he realized he needed another occupation. Secondly, the land he had chosen for his farm, while cheap, had been used hard and most of the best soil had long ago washed into the Cannonsville Reservoir. His final disadvantage, which may have been more crippling than the first two, was that he actually hated cows. Not all the time, mind you, but he especially detested the fact that cows need tending to at least twice a day, every day, three hundred sixty-five days in a year and one of those times was early in the morning. This intense dislike did much to diminish his desire to work with them. Fortunately, at about this time he came to this realization and before he murdered his herd, a broker arrived at his farm and offered him more money for a couple of his rock walls than he could earn in a year of farming. It was thus that Peter found his calling.

After selling off his herd for enough to pay off most of his debt, he still had enough left to buy two used Bobcats and a flatbed truck, which was sufficient equipment to get him started selling stone. Using his knowledge of the local farmers and their land where he had hunted since a preteen, he began buying stone walls, old foundations and rock piles. He then hired some reprobates he knew from living a lifetime in the area to pick and stack the rock on the pallets he constructed in his now, unused barn. Additionally, he was one of the few private rock contractors who actually worked alongside his men, mainly because this line of work allowed him to be both outdoors and independent. Not only did this save him some money, it actually got more work out of his stackers.

Unfortunately, he was not entirely independent. He still had to rely on someone to buy his product and, working as he did in Palatine County, this meant only one outlet: Bisignani Bluestone. While Tom did not offer the highest prices—"Buy low, sell high.", being his motto—it was, for someone willing to work hard, enough to more than get by. Also, Peter had the advantage over most of the other contractors working the county since he owned the heavy equipment, did much of the work himself, and had an "in" with most of the people who owned the land where the rock was located. He was, in a word "reliable", something Tom Bisignani was now to use to his advantage.

After Tom inked the contract to send the two hundred pallets of stone to Hawaii, he immediately thought of Peter Potts as the man to help him meet that commitment. Tom knew that Potts would know where the best place would be to get the stone at this time of year and, once he got it, deliver it on time. Tom immediately contacted the contractor at his Ferrioville farm and got a verbal agreement. Now it was Potts' problem to get the stone out from under the snow and over to Bisignani Bluestone dock by the end of February. It was only to hedge his bet a little that Tom contacted a couple of smaller contractors for a few more pallets to be sure to fill the order.

Fortunately, the good weather and the fact that there was a huge pool of idle men in Palatine County this time of year were working in both Peter and Tom's favor. With the break in the weather, Peter was able to put two crews of five men each into the fields to dig up and load rock at two prime locations. Not knowing how long this weather was going to last, he kept both crews on the job from first light and, often, through to twilight, for six days of the week. (Being a religious man, Peter gave his stackers, but not himself, Sunday off.) The last operation in the day, normally, was loading the previous day's pallets on the flatbed to take to the bluestone dock to be off-loaded and stacked, pallet on pallet, to await the semis, which would haul the pallets to a pier in New York City for transportation. Peter, having acquired some skill in operating a forklift and trying to squeeze a little more profit out of the job, usually did the unloading job by himself rather than pay one of Bisignani's men to do it. So after stacking rock on the pallets all day and using the dusk to dawn yard lights at the dock for illumination, he off-loaded the pallets from his flatbed to the designated spot in the dock. While this saved him money it also added to his day and made him alone responsible for handling the unloading, especially after dark. He also gave himself a little respite by waiting until Sunday night to unload Saturday's pallets.

So it was not surprising to find Peter wheeling round in the muddy gravel of Bisignani's Bluestone dock at nine at night on the second Sunday in February unloading and stacking that Saturday's pallets so he could have the truck back at the collecting site in the morning. This particular Sunday he was in a hurry to get the truck back on site as well, knowing from his years of living in Palatine County that this weather could, despite what the local weatherman was saying, turn in a New

York Minute. The faster the loading was done, the better. Despite the time of night, the southwest winds were keeping the temperatures at a level that was enough to allow one to work up a good sweat. Peter, however, was having some problems with the last pallet in this load.

Friday night in Palatine County is a time to celebrate, especially if you are not well off financially, have worked hard all week and just gotten paid for it. The fact that you may have to go back to your job the next day is not allowed to deter your enjoyment of an evening out and the excessive drinking of alcoholic beverages that go with it. For this reason, those who stacked rock on pallets all week were often a bit hung over when they arrived for work on Saturday morning. While rock stacking is not an exact science, it does require some attention to detail to make sure the rocks are in balance with one another before wrapping the stacked pallet with chicken wire to hold everything in place. If one is not paying attention to what he or she is doing, especially when in the throes of a gigantic, throbbing headache, the balance of the rock may be as tipsy as the stacker was only a few hours before. Normally this is not much of a problem, as once the rock pallets are moved, the rock tends to find its own equilibrium. There are, however, times when this does not happen and one of those times was this Sunday evening.

Peter was tired, this being the sixth time in the last seven days he had been working late at this job, and this one poorly balanced pallet, the last one on the truck, was not cooperating. Try as he might to get it to balance on the top of a two-tier stack, it kept wobbling precariously. To make matters worse, the dock's forklift, since it did not have the lug treads that his Bobcats had, kept slipping and sliding in the mud. He had a fleeting thought that it might be better just to leave the pallet on the ground, but that would mean it would be in the way of traffic in and out of the dock, something he would catch hell from Bisignani for doing. Final, as much by luck as skill, he was able to position the pallet on the top of the pile, where it wobbled a bit and then settled in. Satisfied that it would stay there, he backed the lift truck away, parked it and removed the key. On his way past the office building, he stopped long enough to slip the key through the mail slot in the door so the machine would be available to anyone needing it the next day. It was time for Peter Potts to call it a day. Since this was Sunday and there was no one stacking today, it meant he was done with this part of the job until Tuesday night.

****

BoomBoom had earned some of his commission by setting up the meetings between Weaver and his two buyers. A Thursday check of the "Weekly Planner" on the Weather Channel showed the good weather would be holding at least through the middle of the week of the fifteenth, meaning Monday or Tuesday would be the best time for the trip. That part of the plan assured, BoomBoom first called Bill to see which day would be best for him. Bill said that he did not care but he thought his sister had Monday off so that would be the best day.

Next BoomBoom had called Tom. Tom was okay with Monday but since he had a lot of rock coming in both on Sunday evening and Monday morning, he would prefer any meeting take place later in the afternoon at his stone dock. Not only would this give him time to get his tallying done, but also it would mean the two workers at the dock would be gone for the day. For obvious reasons, he preferred the place be empty at the time of the meeting. This fit in with what BoomBoom had planned since, as long as Jerry was okay with it, they would meet with VanVierden earlier in the day. After getting directions from Tom as to the location of the dock/quarry—not hard since it was right on Route 618 just outside of Snyder's Corners—he hung up and called Jerry.

Jerry had been fine with a late morning/early afternoon meeting. It was ideal for him, in fact. Katrina had already informed him that her golf league meeting was to take place on that Monday morning and she would be gone until early evening. This meant she would not be around while he negotiated the train deal and would not know about it. Jerry preferred it that way since, while the money involved was essentially his, he liked to keep the price of his trains a secret from his spouse. Jerry also gave specific directions from the Stop 'N Go to his house, which he hoped would be easy for BoomBoom to follow.

The only real problem with the Monday meeting was due to BoomBoom's show calendar. He was scheduled to attend an electronics show just outside of Philadelphia that Sunday and, figuring it might be profitable to him, did not want to cancel. That meant if he went all the way down to Philly, he was not going to want to come back home on Sunday night and then drive out again the next morning. Rather he would stay Sunday night in Philly, leave real early on Monday morning to make the three-hour or so hour trip to Snyder's Corners. As a result he would have to make other arrangements to get Bill and Amy to Snyder's Corners. Specifically, Bill would have to drive and they would have to meet some place in the city.

This caused him two problems. The first he would not have the opportunity to spend three hours in the car charming Amy—he had already decided she would ride shotgun with him. The second was a bit more worrisome: he would have to tell Bill where the meeting was to take place. BoomBoom could only hope that by giving out this information so close to the meeting it would prevent Bill from finding out who the buyers were and contacting them to work out a separate deal.

It was not that Bill would have, but it was the nature of BoomBoom's business that he be suspicious of everyone. Like many petty thieves, the deeper they get into crime the more suspicious they became. This suspicion also contributed to another bit of paranoia on BoomBoom's part. To prevent his being robbed of money or merchandise, he had begun, as of late, to carry a pistol. It was a .22 caliber handgun he purchased from one of his street buddies in North Bergen. Being a small model, probably designed for a woman's use, it fit nicely in his jacket pocket and he had taken to carrying it whenever he was toting large amounts of cash. This weekend would be one of those times.

The problem with the pistol was that, as a city boy, BoomBoom had never handled a firearm so had no idea how to shoot it. In fact, other than showing him how to put shells in the magazine neither did the seller. As a consequence, BoomBoom was carrying a loaded .22 caliber handgun without knowing that it had a poorly functioning safety and a hair trigger. Only luck and the fact the chamber was empty prevented him from shooting himself in some part of his anatomy.

With both VanVierden and Bisignani firmed up as to meeting time, BoomBoom had called Bill to tell him the plan. To say that Bill was surprised that the meeting was to take place at Snyder's Corners was an understatement. Bill was hard-pressed not to tell BoomBoom what he knew about the place but just let Cleary fill him in on his plan. In preparation for the meeting, BoomBoom had taken the time to do a MapQuest of Snyder's Corners and picked the Palatine National Bank's parking lot as being the best place to meet Bill and Amy. The two settled on the time just before noon and BoomBoom hung up so Bill could call Amy. BoomBoom had carefully avoided telling Bill who it was they were going to meet, but just told him it would be two separate meetings with two men. That was all he would share.

Thus plans for the meeting were all in place before BoomBoom left North Bergen on Friday night for Philadelphia.

****

Considering the unhappy memories that Amy had about Snyder's Corners, it was understandable if she was uncomfortable about making another trip up there. However, she wanted to be in at the end of this thing so agreed to be ready by nine when Bill came by to pick her up.

****

Monday morning dawned clear and warm. The Channel Four AccuWeather girl was predicting temperatures in the high sixties, maybe even seventy, for Central Park. All of this made Amy surprisingly chipper for someone who headed for, what was perhaps, her most detested place on earth. She was even standing on the curb, ready to go, when Bill pulled up. Bill noted she was wearing a woolen jacket that was going to probably be a little too warm if the predicted temperature was realized.

"Hi Bro. Ready to go?" she asked as he opened the door for her.

"My God, what's with you? Not only are you smiling but you're turned into a poetess. What next, rap?" Bill was happy that his sister was happy; spending six hours in the car with someone who was, at best, morose, was not anything he wanted to do.

"Can't help it. Not only are we going to make a considerable bit of cash and get rid of at least one of my bad memories, its such a nice day."

"Yeah, I'll buy that last part. One thing I hate about getting time off this time of year is the weather is usually so lousy. I can take this weather til spring."

"Oh, don't you still ski?"

"Hell no. That was Phyllis' thing." Bill gave Amy a sideways glance to see how serious she was. "Besides, I'm getting to be too old for that kind of thing."

"Oh yeah, that's right you are getting really old. By the way, did you remember the train?"

"Hey, what are you implying? I might be older than you, but I'm, certainly not senile. It's in the back seat." Bill motioned behind him by jerking his head.

Amy laughed and turned to watch the buildings as they sped by and dropping, for now, the subject of age.

Their trip to Snyder's Corners was uneventful. Aside from a few DOT workers who were taking advantage of the warm weather and foregoing their card games at the state garage by filling potholes with cold patch, there was nothing to hold them up on either the Thruway or Route 17. They made good time and arrived on the outskirts of town a little after eleven. Rather than go to the Tavern for burgers and take another bad trip down memory lane for Amy, Bill pulled into the Stop 'N Go. He bought them both one of the hotdogs that had probably been on the grill's rollers for a week or so. They topped them off with a couple of soft drinks before heading over to the PNB parking lot to meet with BoomBoom

****

BoomBoom's trip up from Philly was equally uneventful. His weekend had been, as expected, profitable for both ends of his business. He had sold the three iPods he had lifted off a loading dock at Best Buy in Paramus and picked up a Dell laptop while the vendors were breaking down on Sunday afternoon. He might have been able to get a few bigger items like speakers or even an amplifier, but since he knew he would not be going directly home from the show, he had left his trailer at his mother's house.

It was now late morning and he was tooling up I-81 above Scranton when he noticed a sign offering fireworks for sale.

It should be noted that Pennsylvania has a unique set of rules when it comes to selling fireworks. Simply put, it is perfectly legal to sell them in the state but illegal to buy them, unless of course you are not a Pennsylvanian. Therefore, vendors set up shop at the Interstate exits close to New York and New Jersey, two states where it is illegal to both sell and possess fireworks. These vendors specifically target the residents of these states who are more than willing to move this contraband across their borders—the vendors even buy TV ads on the out-of-state stations and billboards touting their wares. Anyone can walk into any of these shops, buy anything they wish from sparklers to skyrockets and all they need to leave with the merchandise is the money and a valid out-of- state driver's license. Of course once back in their home state, they could be pulled over by any police agency, given a citation for possession of illegal fireworks, have the products confiscated and be fined, but the chances are so slim of that happening that most find it worthwhile to take their chances. This is all to the profit of the vendors, an increase in Pennsylvania's sales tax revenue, and the delight of attendees at thousands of Fourth of July picnics in these neighboring states.

It was an opportunity for profit, rather than entertaining Independence Day guests that crossed BoomBoom's mind and suggested a scheme. Pulling into the last exit on I-81 that advertised fireworks, he went into the store and loaded up on M-80's, ladyfinger firecrackers, Roman Candles and bottle rockets. He might have rather overdone it in terms of the amount of product he purchased but he was not sure when he would be by here again and wanted to have a variety of stock. The fact that he had money from the electronics show and knew that, once back in North Bergen, he could double or triple it by selling these on the street during in the next four months, was incentive enough for filling the trunk of his car with over five hundred dollars worth of explosives. Besides, he figured that this was the best time of year for moving stuff like this, since the state police would not be especially alert for someone bringing fireworks into the state in February. Moreover, since he was going back to New Jersey by way of New York, it would further throw off suspicion. Overall, he was very happy with himself for making such a shrewd move.

He did make sure, however, to keep well within the legal speed limit on the rest of the trip to Snyder's Corners—no sense in tempting the cops. He arrived just in time to see Bill's car pull into the PNB parking lot. Bill got out of his car and walked over to BoomBoom's. Amy stayed where she was.

— Chapter 13 —

JERRY VANVIERDEN DID NOT feel well when he awoke on February fifteenth. While he could not exactly pin down the cause, he had a nagging feeling that something was not right in his bladder and urinary tract. His usual, first thing in the morning, piss was less than satisfactory both in strength of stream and quantity. It briefly crossed his mind that this might be signaling some kind of prostate problem but, slipping into denial, he dismissed it. Rather, he laid it off to the fact that he had not been in to see Madame Orey in the last two months and, more than likely; it was being caused by anxiety about the upcoming train deal. At any rate, he brushed it off and did not say anything to Katrina. As soon as she left, he would call the Madam and make an appointment.

Katrina left for her meeting at the country club a little before eleven. This gave Jerry time before the meeting with BoomBoom to make the call to Orey. The Madame said that she had an opening that afternoon; something that Jerry would be unable to make due to his meeting with BoomBoom and the sellers. He was, however, able to get his name on the schedule for Wednesday at two. Jerry had just hung up the phone as a car came up the long driveway from Route 618.

****

Bill was impressed by the house they were approaching. It was built against the east side of the hill where the view of sunsets must have been spectacular and had plenty of glass so the residents could enjoy them. No question that whoever lived there could afford the price of the train he held on his lap. Bill, who had been relegated to the backseat when BoomBoom offered the front seat to Amy, had to wait for her to get out of the car. *Damn two-door cars,* he thought, *they're not made for old guys.*

BoomBoom led the way to the front door and, checking to see that Bill and Amy were close behind him rang the bell. Jerry answered almost immediately.

"Good morning, BoomBoom." Jerry was the first to speak, knowing as he did the eBay seller from their face-to-face meetings in York. The fact that the time was a little after the noon hour meant the morning greeting was close enough. "I trust you had a good trip."

"Yeah, no problems. I want you to meet Amy and Bill. They're the ones with the train." BoomBoom was not much with the niceties of etiquette and just gestured in the direction of Amy and Bill who had followed him in from the car. He also figured it was not necessary to divulge last names as they were not important.

"Pleased to meet you, I'm Jerry VanVierden." Jerry offered his hand to Amy, who, he noted was a tall, stunning blond. "And you." The greeting to Bill was almost an afterthought. "Please come in."

"I'm Bill and this is my sister, Amy," Bill responded, unnecessarily since it was obvious who was who. He did not see any reason why he needed to give last names either. Besides, he was not sure what Amy was using for her last name now anyway.

Jerry ushered the three into the front hall of his house. "May I take your coats?" he asked, then, noting the package under Bill's arm. "Is that the train?"

"Yes it is." Bill helped Amy out of her coat and handed her the package so he could remove his. He handed both coats to Jerry who placed them on hangers and hung them in the entry's closet. BoomBoom,

Bill noticed, was wearing only a light jacket and opted to keep it on. Taking the train from his sister, he asked. "Is there someplace we can sit down so you can look at this set?"

"Sure. I thought you might like to see my train layout so let's go down into my train room. There is a table and chairs down there where we can be comfortable." Jerry motioned to the door leading to the lower level of the house. "Is there anything I can get for you, something to eat, coffee?"

"No, we're quite alright. We just ate in town but thank you." It was now Amy's turn to reply. Following Jerry's lead, she descended the stairs. Bill, carrying the train, was right behind her. BoomBoom brought up the rear.

"Oh!" Again it was Amy who was first to react to the sight of Jerry's layout.

Jerry had earlier taken the time to turn on the lights to display the models at their best. Although nothing was operating, he had also turned up the voltage on the transformers so he could, at a moments notice, program in a locomotive and fire it up if his visitors wanted to see the layout in operation. He was not sure how much the seller would know about trains but as he did when anyone came into his train room, he wanted to be ready to show off his work. He was beaming at the fact Amy was impressed.

"It looks like you've got yourself a few trains here." Bill, while as impressed as his sister, was trying to act blasé.

"It is a layout I've worked on for a long time, that's for sure." Then in an attempt to make a further impact on his guest, Jerry added. "I don't have everything out on the tracks either. A lot of it is stored in those dehumidified cabinets under the table. In fact, I've just gotten back from vacation and really haven't gotten everything out I normally have on the layout."

"Looks like a lot here to me." Bill, still holding the Lionel locomotive, moved closer to examine the layout. He reached out rather absently mindedly as if he were going to touch the track.

"I wouldn't do that if I were you." Jerry warned. "That track is hot and, while it wouldn't produce enough of a shock to do any more than startle you, it might give you a surprise."

Bill jerked his hand back. "Thanks for the warning."

"How's about we get down to business?" This was the first BoomBoom had spoken since the introductions out in front of the house. BoomBoom was interested in getting this deal done, not in seeing any trains run around in circles.

"Of course. Please sit down." Jerry motioned to a round, poker type table that sat near the stairs. There were three seats around it. Bill, Amy and BoomBoom took the seats while Jerry drew up the bar-type of stool with the MTH logo on it where he sat when running his layout. This meant when he was seated he was higher than the other three. Somehow, he felt this gave him an advantage.

With everyone seated, Jerry said. "Now, let's see the prize."

Bill placed the mailing box on the table and carefully slid the inner carton out. Once it was free, he placed the box on the floor beside his chair and handed the train in its display box to Jerry.

Jerry, bending down from his perch, took the box, slowly turned it while examining the contents through the cut-out window. "May I take it out?" he asked.

"I haven't removed it from the box in order to keep it as new as possible. But, I guess if you're gonna want to buy it, you might's well take a close look." was Bill's response.

As carefully as he could, Jerry opened the end flap and, grasping the inner cardboard carrier between his thumb and forefinger, tugged until this train cradle slid free. In a matter of seconds, the locomotive and tender were free of the box. Jerry held it up and using both hands, brought it closer to him. Slowly he turned it in front of his face for a closer inspection.

The first thing Jerry noticed was that, for the age of the loco, it was well done. The casting was exquisite, probably done using new molds then followed by a lot of handwork to bring out detail. While, in terms of modern work, this detail was crude, for the nineteen twenties it was a masterpiece. For whatever reason, Lionel had outdone itself producing this one.

"It's beautiful. An especially well done piece." Jerry carefully reinserted the carrying carton back in the box and handed it back to Bill. Bill ducked down and retrieved the mailing box. "Lionel must certainly have taken its time to produce that one."

"The way I understand it, this was supposed to be a special run just for Lionel dealers. From the information I got from my contact in the Train Collectors Association, there were only fifty of these made in 1929 and this is one of only four accounted for." Bill wanted to make sure Jerry knew he had done his homework on this item and knew its value. In actuality, Bill knew considerably more than Jerry did on this account since the only thing Jerry knew about the model was what Tom had told him over the phone. Tom had been deliberately vague when describing the originality of the item to him.

"I see. That would make it very valuable then." Furrowing his brow and looking down at Bill, Jerry asked. "How much are we talking here?"

"At least ten thousand." Bill responded with a number that seemed within the amount Farmer told him it was worth.

"Ten thousand." Jerry's response was neither a question nor a confirmation but just a repeat of Bill's amount. Bill noticed, however, that if the amount surprised VanVierden he did not show it. "From what you have told me and from what I can see, I would say that is a reasonable price."

Bill looked first at Amy and then at BoomBoom and, since neither responded, he went on. "I must warn you, you are not the only person interested in it. We have another person, right here in town as a matter of fact, who is interested and wants to make an offer. I'd say we're obligated to see him as well."

Jerry smiled. "That would undoubtedly be my friend Thomas." For some reason Jerry used the full name for Tom, not the short version. "I'm not at all surprised. Not only is he the only person around with an interest in trains and the money to make an offer that high for one, but I know he has dealt with BoomBoom and is a big Lionel collector. I take it you haven't talked to him yet."

"Not yet." BoomBoom answered. "We're gonna go to his place soon as we leave here."

"So, what does that mean about the selling price for this?" Jerry wanted to know.

"I haven't really thought about it. Have you?" Bill nodded in BoomBoom's direction.

Actually, BoomBoom had not thought it though either since he was not one to think that far ahead. This meant he had to do some immediately seat-of-the-pants thinking. He began slowly, using his eBay experience, and making it up as he went. "Well.... I assume we'd let Jerry, here, give us a bid. Then we'll go see the other buyer and see what he'll bid. Whoever is higher gets the train. We should be able to close the deal sometime before supper."

"As long as the highest bid is in the range we want for the train." Bill added.

"Yeah, sure." BoomBoom had not considered that.

"Sounds reasonable as long as each of us has one bid. I would hate to make you an offer and then have you tell the other buyer what it is so he can top it. That hardly seems fair. And I really don't want to turn this into a bidding war where someone snipes a last second bid."

"I agree. We don't want to turn it into that either and we're not in this to screw anyone." Bill was being completely honest. Also, he wanted to get this train sold today. He did not want to have to come back to Snyder's Corners again and was sure that Amy felt the same way.

"I know what we can do." It was Amy with a suggestion. "You put your bid on a folded piece of paper and give it to BoomBoom. Then when we get to this other buyer, we'll have him do the same thing. When we have both offers, BoomBoom will compare the two and whoever's the higher gets the set." Amy was not aware that BoomBoom had any stake in the sale except for the commission she and Bill were paying them.

"Sounds good to me." Jerry nodded. Getting off the stool, he went to the desk along the wall on the other side of the room, took out a piece of note paper, wrote down a number, folded it and, returning, handed it to BoomBoom. BoomBoom put it in his shirt pocket.

"Thank you for your time." Bill pushed back from the table, stood and picked up the box with the train.

"Pleasure was all mine." Jerry was smiling and looking directly at Amy. "I hope you will be back to deliver my train."

Following them upstairs, Jerry went to the closet, retrieved the coats and handed Bill his and then helped Amy into hers. She tossed her hair back over the collar in such a way as it brushed his hand.

"Thanks again." Bill shook Jerry's hand and taking Amy's arm guided her out to the car. He did not notice that BoomBoom stayed back and had a couple of quiet words with Jerry.

"Geeze" Bill whispered to Amy as the approached the car, "did you have to come on to him?"

"I didn't have to but he seemed like a nice guy. Who knows, maybe it got us an extra couple of dollars." Amy smiled, waited for Bill to get into the back seat, then slid into the front seat and put on the seatbelt. BoomBoom, who just reached the car, glanced over trying to see how far the skirt she was wearing would slide up her thighs. Bill just chuckled and shook his head.

As soon as he heard the car door close, Jerry, suffering a series of bladder spasms, sprinted to the bathroom. He managed only a few dribbles. He was beginning to worry.

Once down the driveway, BoomBoom stopped to check the directions Tom had given him then headed back up Route 618, passed the Stop 'N Go toward Tom's bluestone dock. Glancing at his watch, and seeing it was after one o'clock, found himself hoping they were not going to be too early.

****

Tom had been nervous most of the morning. He hurriedly made a count of the pallets Potts had stacked the night before and waited for the two loads that were scheduled to be brought in by other dealers that day. Fortunately, both came in at about the same time, earlier than expected and were small enough that his two yardmen, Jess and Ray, got them unloaded and stacked quickly. Then, even though it was shortly after noon and since there was nothing else scheduled for the three of them to do for the rest of the day, he gave both yardmen the rest of the day off. He also told them that he would be sticking around to do some paper work. In actually, all he really had to do was to wait for BoomBoom.

Amy had not really been paying attention to where they were going, just being locked into her own thoughts as the scenery rolled by the car window. When BoomBoom slowed the car to make an approach to the entrance of the bluestone dock, she snapped out of her self-imposed trance and looked up just in time to see the sign: Bisignani Bluestone, Thomas Bisignani Owner. She let out an audible gasp.

Bill heard his sister's cry from his position in the back seat and thought for a minute that she might be carsick, maybe from the hot dog. Worried, he leaned over the seat to check if she was okay and seeing no visible problem, relaxed. He did, however, follow her stare in the direction of the sign, read it, but did not make any connection.

The car made a squishing noise as it splashed through the muddy water in the yard. Pulling up in front of the shed that served as an office, BoomBoom shut off the key and got out just as Tom Bisignani came out the office door. Tom acknowledged BoomBoom immediately but did not recognize the blond slowly getting out of the other side of the car.

— Chapter 14 —

It had been over twenty-five years since Tom had last seen Amy, so there was no reason he would have or should have recognized her. Besides there had been many girls her age and younger before and after her, not counting those he had hired on his trips to Thailand. To him, she had been just something to use and discard.

On the other hand, there was every reason for her to remember him, and she did as soon as he walked out of the office.

BoomBoom was the first to step out of the car after it sloshed to a stop in front of the dock's office. Unprepared for the mud, he sunk to his ankles in the red, wet stuff and then almost left his sneakers behind as he tried to extract his feet from the goo.

"God Damn it!" BoomBoom's disgust only got a smile from Tom who was standing on the porch in mud-covered, knee-high boots. "What kinda shit is this?"

"Welcome to springtime in the Catskills, BoomBoom." Tom said, "I take it these are the sellers."

As Tom spoke, Amy and Bill disembarked very gingerly from the opposite side of the car. Forewarned by BoomBoom's experience, both were looking for and not being successful at finding, dry spots to place their feet. Gingerly and as best they could, they made their way toward the dry porch.

"Yeah, that's them," BoomBoom, having slogged his way to some less muddy ground indicated Amy and Bill who had now picked their way to the porch. "Amy and Bill." This was all there was of BoomBoom's introduction since he figured Tom could figure out which one was which.

Tom nodded. Like Jerry, he had not expected two people, much less a man and woman, but he did not show any surprise either. "I'm Tom Bisignani.," he said reaching out to offer his hand to first Amy and then Bill.

"Yes I know." Amy took the Tom's hand and then, curiously, looked hard into his face. Tom missed the implication entirely.

Bill shook the hand offered but still had not spoken. Rather he was looking down at the mud layering his shoes and wondering if they would ever be the same again. He was carrying the long, brown cardboard mailing package under his arm. He also missed Amy's remark entirely.

"Please come in." Tom caught a look from Amy, but did not pick up on it. He opened the door to his office and ushered his three guests inside. "May I take your coats?"

"Nah, I'm fine," BoomBoom declined. He tapped his feet on the office floor, trying to dislodge some of the mud packed into the tread of the sneakers. All it did was leave a red streaked mark on the floor.

"Me too." said Bill, hoping that this part of the meeting would not take long enough for the heat inside the building to cause him any discomfort. Besides, his feet were wet and he expected the chill to pass onto the rest of his body. Bill noticed that Tom had not removed his coat either.

"Yes, thank you." Much to Bill's disgust, Amy allowed Tom to help her remove her coat. Once again Bill figured Amy was trying to use her body to sweeten the deal. This was not her intention. Rather she hoped that with Tom having to come this close to her, it would spark some glimmer of recognition. It did not. He only had eyes for the package under Bill's arm.

"That the loco?" Tom asked once he had hung Amy's coat on the coat tree by the door.

"Yes." Bill replied, removing the box from under his arm. "Can I use this table to set it down to open it?" Bill indicated a flat-topped table that served as the main desk in the office. Normally covered with tally sheets and order blanks, Tom had used the time while he waited to clear it of everything but the company computer.

"By all means." While Bill stepped to the table, noting the squishing from his shoes, Tom went around to the opposite side in anticipation.

As he had at Jerry's house, Bill slid the insert box out of the mailing box and held it up for all to see. Slowly turning it so Tom could see the locomotive and tender through the cut-out window, Bill asked. "Would you like to take it out?"

"Of course." Tom hoped his voice did not betray his excitement.

Then, in an unexpected move and before taking the box from Bill, Tom took out a pair of white cotton gloves from his coat pocket and put them on. He followed by taking the box, setting it on the table in front of him and opening it. Removing the cardboard carrier, he lifted the locomotive from it with his gloved hands. Looking at Bill, whose body language may have betrayed a question, he smiled and said, "I don't want to get finger prints on this."

Bill nodded his head and thought, *This guy is either very careful or a kook.*

Tom's inspection of the locomotive and tender was lengthier and more loving than the one Jerry had done. His eyes went over every detail of the loco, how it was put together, the connection between the tender and the engine and then to the tender itself. He examined each feature from the lettering on the tender to the hand mounted piping on the engine with a tested and loving eye. Tom could not help but think back to whomever had done the work, the time and skill that had gone into every part to make them fit so well together. *True artisans made this.*, he thought. *Lionel had made better but not in the twenties.*

Tom had never scrutinized any of the women or girls in his life to the depth that he did this train set. Had he done so, he would have probably remembered Amy. By the time he finally placed the piece back on the table, he knew there was no way in the world he was going to let it leave this building except to go home with him. Ever so slowly, he replaced the locomotive and tender on the carrier and reinserted them into the display carton.

The way he had lovingly fondled the set and returned it to its box was so erotic that it was surprising the males in the room had not seemed to notice it. Amy, however, most assuredly did. As a woman, she knew that look, the caress, and that final thrust. This man had just made love with that locomotive. Someplace, deep inside her, she felt a twinge of remembrance that jolted her.

As soon as he returned the set to the box and unable to hold it in any longer, Amy asked, "You don't remember me do you?" As she spoke, she placed her hand on the gloved hand holding the box and looked straight at Tom.

"Should I?" He was slowly coming out of the erotic trance brought on by fondling the train. Now he awoke, confused as to why this woman was holding his hand and staring at him.

"I thought not. I am, err was, Amy Weaver." Amy was still staring up at Tom, hoping the name would evoke some recognition.

"Amy Weaver." There was a pause then a flicker and finally a recollection. "Oh yes, William Lawyer's niece. It's been a long time." Something he had put behind him long ago and had successfully repressed was coming back.

"Long time? Tom it's been almost twenty-five years!"

"Jesus Christ!" Bill had been listening to the conversation between Tom and Amy and it finally hit him. "This is Tom?"

"He knows?" Tom looked from Amy to Bill and back to her. He was trying to remember details, but they were not coming back that quickly.

"Yeah, he knows. I told him how some old guy screwed his fourteen-year old sister for a summer!" Amy had raised her voice. She was now feeling some deep emotion but she was not sure what. Was it anger that Tom had not recognized her or sadness at what had been lost back then? No, it was something else. She had just seen Tom show more passion for that train than he ever showed during that summer with her. Seeing it made her realize that what she had had with him was not, as she thought, love but sex, sex where he was using her, sex meant to humiliate her, sex to satisfy himself. That sudden realization turned her stomach and suddenly all she wanted was to get out of there, out of that building, out of the deal and out of Palatine County.

She got to her feet. As she did, she reached across the table and grabbed the boxed train. "We're getting put of here!" She said grabbing the box and pulling it back across the table toward her.

"What?" Bill was with his sister but not exactly sure what she was doing.

"You can't have that!" Tom, his reflexes a bit slower, tried to grab the train back from Amy.

"Oh yes I can. It's mine. I inherited it from my uncle and I not gonna let some old lecher have it!" Amy now had the train set and was starting for the door.

"No you're not." They had all been ignoring BoomBoom who was standing next to the door. He was now blocking it. He had his hand in his jacket pocket.

Through Tom's inspection of the train, BoomBoom, because he could not hear the conversation, had not been paying that much attention, rather he was just standing back and waiting for the final negotiation to take place. Jerry had told him in private just before they left his house that the bid on the paper had been eleven hundred dollars but if BoomBoom were able to get it for less, any extra would go to him in addition to five hundred as a finder's fee. On the trip over from Jerry's, BoomBoom was trying to figure how he could get more from Bisignani. He was still mulling that over in his mind when he heard Amy shout something about "some old guy screwed his fourteen-year old sister". He looked up just in time to see her grab the boxed train away from Tom and bolt for the door. All he knew now was if he did not stop her he might be out a lot of money.

"Everyone's staying right here." BoomBoom tried to use his most authoritarian voice. He hoped the pistol that now was in his hand added to that.

He got Bill's attention.

Seeing BoomBoom positioned in the doorway with a gun in his hand, Bill grabbed Amy by the arm and held her back. "Sis, what's going on?" He looked closely at Amy's face and all he saw was anger.

"I don't want him to have this." She indicated the set in her hand. "He doesn't deserve it. He's just a dirty old man who uses young girls." Somehow, seeing his actions with the train had made it clear to her.

When Bill spun Amy around, it gave Tom the space and time needed to get by her and place himself next to BoomBoom at the door. The look on Tom's face only reinforced BoomBoom's position.

"Give me that train." Tom stepped forward and made a lunge for the box. Amy, smaller and quicker, dodged out of the way and made a dash for the other end of the small office.

BoomBoom, forgetting his job was to guard the door, tried to head Amy off. She slipped by him and then, hoping her brother was paying attention, tossed the box high in the air in his direction. "Bill, catch!"

Bill looked up just in time to see the train set inches from his head. Reactions he had used as a tight end in high school football and did not know he still had, took over. He reached up and grabbed the box out of the air. Noticing the door was unguarded; he opened it and rushed outside—for all he knew heading for the end zone.

This created one problem, once outside he had no idea where he was going to go. Not that it made any difference.

"Hold it!" The command came from Tom Bisignani. Bill turned, feeling cool mud from the parking lot oozing into his shoes, to see Tom holding his sister by one arm. He had BoomBoom's pistol pressed to her head and there was an audible click as Tom chambered a round. Bill could see Amy's eyes and she was not as much frightened as angry. "Come back here."

Slowly Bill slogged back though the mud to the office porch. Automatically, he tucked the box holding the train under his arm.

BoomBoom was confused, first the turmoil in the office, then Tom taking the gun from him and putting it to Amy's head. He had not planned on the whole thing coming down to this and was beginning to wonder if he had not made some mistake. Of even more concern to him was that he might be out his finder's fee.

"Looks like I just bought a collectible Lionel train." Tom was gloating. "And at my price too."

"Like hell you have." Amy was, even with the barrel of the .22 pressed to her temple, defiant. "We're not going to sell it to you so if you take it, you're stealing it. We'll turn you in to the cops."

"Cops? Honey, this is Palatine County, we don't have cops. We have a sheriff and he just happens to be a Republican. Guess, sweetheart, who is head of the Republican Party in Palatine County?" Bill was still smiling.

"I bet it is you, you son of a bitch."

"Right, but I really don't want a whore like you ruining my reputation now do I? So I guess I'll have to go to plan B."

"Plan B?" BoomBoom was beginning to get a little more worried.

"Probably it isn't going to turn out too good for us." Amy said.

"You guessed it sister." Tom turned to BoomBoom, "I'm gonna need your help."

"My help?" BoomBoom genuinely had not caught on.

"Yeah, you want your finder's fee, don't you?"

"Yeah sure." BoomBoom was glad he was not going to lose that even though he was not sure yet what he would have to do to earn it since it sounded like the sale was off.

"I've got a two hundred-foot deep quarry at the back of this dock that is half filled with water and a lot of rock lying around. We'll just drop these two in with some of that rock for weight and they'll never be found. "

"You're talking about killing them?" Somehow, the thought had not crossed BoomBoom's mind. Now that it was out there, he did not seem to have the qualms he would have thought he would. All he could think about was that he hoped this would make his fee bigger.

"What does it sound like to you?" Amy was trying to see if, somehow she could get at the gun. "What are you, some kind of an idiot?" She spat out the words as much to BoomBoom as to Tom.

Not hearing an objection from BoomBoom, Tom pushed Amy off the porch into the mud. He indicated that Bill should precede them toward the back of the dock and passed the stacked rock. The quarry, abandoned several years ago because it was filling with water, was located behind the load storage area of the dock.

Because of the mud and the fact that Amy was not being very cooperative, the pace was slow. It had taken several minutes for them just to get to where the stacks of pallets for shipment to Hawaii were located. Although the mud was deep and made movement difficult, Tom was in good enough shape that he was the one keeping Amy moving. As they reached this part of the dock, Tom realized they had left Amy's coat back in the office. He did not want that around as it might cause someone to ask questions so he sent BoomBoom back to get it while they waited.

"You bastard. How could you treat me like this? We had something going back twenty-five years ago." Even with the gun at her head, Amy had managed to squirm in Tom's grasp so she could face him.

" Something going? You gotta be kidding. You were just a nice young piece of ass as far as I was concerned. Hell, until today I hadn't even giving you a thought since I last screwed you."

"You mean there were others?"

"Hell yes. You weren't even the first or the youngest. Up until I remarried I had a twelve to fifteen-year old living with me most every summer, sometimes all year long. Wasn't you, it would have been somebody else."

"You must have been something. How the hell did you get away with it?" Bill, who was a few feet past the pile of rock, turned to ask this question.

Tom stood, his back to the pallets of rock destined for Hawaii, feeling his feet sink into the mud. He was proud of himself and the fact that for a period of over twenty years he had used young girls and had gotten away with it. "Son, this is Palatine County. In this county, there are lotsa families that have girls that aren't happy. Most of them get abused by their daddies, step-daddies or mama's boyfriend and if there is a chance for them to pick up a little money on the side they're quite willing to go along with an old guy that's willing to pay. It's just that simple. Certainly, the girls or their parents didn't mind. I helped them out financially is all, didn't cost me much. Combine that with the fact that the sheriff is in my pocket and too stupid to ask questions; there is nobody around who would much care." Pausing to look Amy up and down, he continued. "I will say that you've aged better than most of them. What are you, late thirties? By the time most of the others reached that age they've been knocked up five or six times and lost all their teeth."

"Yeah, that might be true." Amy said "But I sure as hell didn't cost you anything to do me, aside from a cheap piece of jewelry."

"That diamond broach wasn't exactly cheap." Some of their relationship was coming back to him. "But, if the truth be known, you cost me plenty with your Uncle."

"Uncle William!?" Both Amy and Bill said it simultaneously.

"Yup, your Uncle William. Not only did I pay him a few hundred bucks, but I got him a couple of political appointed jobs that earned him a nice pension. He was able to shut down that sorry ass, money losing hardware store of his and retire on those pensions."

"You mean to tell me that Uncle William was pimping me that summer?"

"Sure was. Did a good job of it too. No one ever found out."

"Why you son of a bitch!" While Tom was bragging, he had relaxed just enough to allow Amy to manage to pull lose from his grip and come full face with him. Anger showed in not only her face but also in every fiber of her body. That rage now generated almost superhuman strength. Being lighter than Tom, she had not sunk as deeply into the mud as he, thus she was able to lift her knee up into his groin with a lot of force unimpeded by the mud's suction.

Tom's feet were anchored solidly in the mud so the blow to his testicles, which he could do nothing to avoid, caused an immediate amount of pain. In reaction to this pain, his knees bent but, as his feet were locked in place by the mud, this caused him to lose his balance and fall backward into the pallet that was just behind him. The force of his body hitting this lowest pallet in the stack set off a chain reaction. As he staggered back, he also released Amy's wrist the rest of the way.

During the months of December and January, the ground in the dock had frozen rock solid down to a depth of eighteen inches. With the warm weather of the past week, the top six or so inches had defrosted—driving the frost down as the old timers called it—making this upper layer soft. While the pallets that Peter Potts unloaded the day before had settled into these six inches and stabilized, they also carried some latent heat that melted the ground a little deeper. In addition, the rock facing the sun on the pallets also warmed during that day, passing this heat down in such a way that the ground under the front edge of the pallets became softer down a little deeper than the ground on the back, shaded part. Since Tom Bisignani had fallen against this front edge, his extra weight drove this edge deeper into the mud. As this edge was now considerably lower than the back, it caused the stack to tip in his direction.

This movement also dislodged a rock on the top of the poorly stacked pallet, which Potts had had a hard time balancing on the third layer of that stack. This rock rolled forward causing the other poorly stacked rocks on the same pallet to move with it in the same direction. Like the first snowball in an avalanche, the movement of that first rock caused the whole stack to lose equilibrium and topple forward. Because each rock and pallet below it was so tightly packed, their combined weight brought the whole stack with them. In less time that it takes to tell it, there was over half a ton of rock coming down on Tom Bisignani and Amy.

Bill saw it coming, did not have time to shout a warning but was able, again using the reactions he no long knew he had, to grab Amy's arm and yank her out of harm's way. Tom, being closer to the stack, his feet mired in the mud, had no chance of escape. In an instant, the rock, chicken wire and wooden pallets cascaded down on Tom Bisignani, pile driving him facedown into the soft mud, only to abruptly stop once his body hit the frozen ground underneath. Had the combined weight not crushed his spine and killed him instantly, he certainly would have suffocated from having mud forced into his nostrils. Only one, cotton-gloved hand sticking grotesquely out at right angles to the pile indicated there was someone under it.

Assured that Amy was out of harm's way and okay, Bill, kneeled down in the mud, and felt for a pulse in that wrist. There was none. He looked up to see BoomBoom standing several feet away, holding Amy's coat out at an angle, with a dumbfounded look on his face. Bill rose and took a step toward BoomBoom, not sure what he was about to do but knowing it was not going to be pleasant.

BoomBoom, recognizing Bill's intention as one he had seen as a youth and not being willing to protect himself from a sure beating, dropped Amy's coat in the mud, turned and, slipping and sliding, ran to his car. Once started, he made a Huey in the parking lot and, spewing mud and rock drove out on the highway headed back toward town and New Jersey.

"Let him go. We can deal with him later." Amy spoke from where she was sitting on a pallet of rock, her shoes, dress and face spattered with red mud. "Let's get the hell outa here."

"Ok, how?" As Bill spoke, he bent down, retrieved her coat and brought it to her.

"Remember I told you I used to wander around in the woods?"

Bill nodded.

"Well, if I remember correctly, there's a path that leads from the other side of the quarry, down along a steam, and comes out near the courthouse. It's only a couple of blocks from there to the bank."

"Ok, you lead. I'll follow. Let's go."

Amy took the coat, wrapped it around her shoulders and led her brother through the stacks of palleted rock to the edge of the quarry and down the hill. It took them about thirty minutes to get back to Bill's car. It was only when he started to reach for his keys that Bill realized he still had the train set under his arm. The mailing carton, however, had been left back at the dock's office. He handed the train set to Amy as he got into the car and started it.

— Chapter 15 —

ASIDE FROM GETTING AS far away from Bill Weaver as possible, the other thing on BoomBoom's mind was that he was now out any money on this deal. As he sped down Route 618 toward town, this second thought made him a bit sad but he rationalized that at least Bill and Amy had no connection to him except through his mother. Assuming they both survived—something BoomBoom was not sure would happen since he had visions of something attacking and eating them in the woods—he was confident they would be glad they were rid of him and could not do him any harm. He would just have to get back to New Jersey before them and make sure his mother understood the importance of keeping his whereabouts secret.

Coming up on the Stop 'N Go, BoomBoom noticed his gas gauge indicated he was low on fuel. Not wanting to make another stop before he got back to North Bergen, he figured it would be best to fill up now, so he pulled into the pump furthest from the store. Reaching down to the lever to open his gas cap he accidentally tripped the wrong one, opening the trunk instead, then, realizing his mistake, he yanked up on the second, gas cap, lever. As he got out of the car, he reminded himself to close the trunk before he pulled out. As bad as things had already gone, he did not want it compounded by having someone spot the fireworks.

It is said that if a man is illiterate and cannot read this is a tragic. At the same time, if a man is literate and does not read, it is a tragedy. BoomBoom was to fall in the second of these groups.

What he did not bother to read was the sign on the gas pump that said:

Warning: Fire Hazard

Static Electricity may ignite

Gasoline vapors.

When filling portable containers

Do Not fill any portable container

In or on a vehicle.

Do Not use cell phones

When dispensing gasoline.

After swiping his credit card, starting the pump, and, just as he was about to place the nozzle into the filler tube, he heard his cell phone in his jacket pocket ring. In trying to juggle the nozzle and reach for the phone, he accidentally spilt about half a gallon of gasoline onto the top of the car's rear fender. Because the trunk was partly open, some of this gas managed to trickle down into the seam where the trunk lid met the rear fender. Once he managed to retrieve the phone, but before he could answer it, he also thrust the nozzle into the gas tank filler and started the flow of gas into the tank. Just then the phone rang a second time. As luck would have it, the area of the Stop 'N Go was one of the few places in Palatine County where there was a clear cell phone signal.

It had been an especially unseasonably warm, dry, and windless day and the pumps at the Stop 'N Go were located in such a way that they were directly in the afternoon sun. Coupled with the canopy over the pumps, which further limited air movement, the temperatures around the pumps reached a level that caused the gasoline to vaporize. Given the lack of air movement these gasoline fumes were trapped near the pumps. Since BoomBoom's phone was close to the place where he had spilt the gasoline and the fumes were especially intense there, the electrical spark generated by the second phone ring was just enough to ignite these fumes. The resulting flame spread to the spill.

Like most self-serve stations, the Stop 'N Go had devices in place that would kick in under just this kind of emergency. First, the pumps automatically shut off, and then retardant, sprayed from nozzles in the canopy, would douse the fire. Had these steps been able to be followed, BoomBoom might have escaped with only minor first and second degree burns to his hand and arm. However, there were extenuating circumstances that caused this fire to spread faster than the automatic system was designed to react to it.

From the initial flash of fire, the flame crept down the stream of spilled gasoline into the trunk and ignited the cardboard carton holding the first box of fireworks—the M-80's—which were closest to the trunk opening and had been soaked with fuel. As the carton caught fire, the flame reached the fuses of the firecrackers inside and ignited all of them simultaneously. In addition, the confined space of the car's trunk contained the fire in such a way that it allowed it to spread to the other cartons, igniting them and, very quickly, reaching the fuses of the merchandise they contained. The results were immediate and spectacular.

First, the whole box of M-80's exploded. The explosion blew open the unlatched car trunk, created enough concussion to blow out the gasoline fire but, at the same time, shredding BoomBoom into small pieces. Next, the Roman candles and bottle rockets began to flying off into space through the now opened trunk. Some of these lodged in the canopy above, effectively destroying the automatic dousing system. With balls of flame from the candles and streaking rockets going in every direction, secondary fires started in the Stop 'N Go as well as Maggie's Diner across the street. One rocket, which gained entry to the convenience store where the main window had disintegrated in the explosion, landed in the display of Dolly Madison snack cakes and set them ablaze, setting off the store's sprinkler system. A ball of flame from a Roman candle set the cartons of washer fluid stacked in front of the store afire, melting the plastic bottles, which allowed the fluid to run all over the parking lot. This rocket attack following the explosion and including the rat-tat tat reports of the ladyfingers going off convinced the Stop 'N Go clerk that he was under a terrorist attack. He dove for the floor behind the counter, covered his head, and stayed there until the first volunteer fireman into the store managed to pry him loose.

In Maggie's, because the windows there were also gone, a bottle rocket landed in the deep fryer setting the oil ablaze. Only the quick thinking of a cook, who grabbed the fire extinguisher, saved the diner and prevented a more serious calamity. In one of the rigs parked next to the diner, the explosion startled one of the working girls who was at that moment fellating one of the big rig's drivers so badly that she almost caused serious damage to the trucker she was servicing.

The whole event lasted, probably, no more than three minutes. By the time it was over, two other cars that had been parked at the other set of pumps were smoldering, the interior of the Stop 'N Go store was ablaze, and the pumps nearest to where BoomBoom's car—now a charred hulk—had been parked were flattened. It was fortunate that, excepting for BoomBoom, there were no other serious injuries. Aside from a few scrapes that resulted in their diving for cover, the other customers at the pumps and in the store had managed to get out of harm's way. (The trucker had a bruise that, while it was to cause him a bit of discomfort when he urinated for the next week or so, would heal. The girl needed six stitches to close the wound on the back of her head where she hit the underside of the steering wheel.) Miraculously, even the glass shards, pieces of flying metal and shooting flames had missed everyone. The first law officer, a county sheriff's deputy, to arrive on the scene and a veteran of the Iraq War, said the devastation looked like the results of a roadside bomb.

It took the Snyder's Corners volunteer fire company about half an hour to put out the fires in the convenience store and to secure the area so someone could try to find the cause of it. After Palatine County Sheriff Bill Pierce arrived, he put in a call to the New York State Police asking that they send in a CSI team to try to figure out what had happened. Since he was sure a bomb had gone off, the Sheriff was hoping the scene would be cleaned up before someone tipped off the Bureau of Alcohol and Firearms, as, like most local law officials, he did not want feds crawling all over his territory. One could never be too sure what the ATF would turn up.

The state CSI team found bits and pieces of BoomBoom, some embedded in the side of the Stop 'N Go. Among these parts was his charred hand that still was gripping what was left of his melted cell phone. Able to lift a thumbprint from the hand and, in conjunction with the twisted license plate from BoomBoom's car, they were able to positively identify his body very quickly. (Ironically, the matching print was on file because as a child, his mother had had him fingerprinted at a lost children clinic when he was six.) This enabled Sheriff Pierce to place a call to the North Bergen police department so they could notify the next of kin.

****

Jerry VanVierden was anxious about both the train set and his inability to pee. Earlier he had tried to call BoomBoom's cell phone but after two rings, he was cut off. He had tried again later but it did not even ring. (An explosion that rattled the windows in Jerry's house followed the first try, but he just assumed it was coming from one of the quarries.) More worrisome was that since BoomBoom, Amy and Bill had left, Jerry's bladder had stretched to capacity and, no matter how hard he strained, nothing would come out. The pain was reaching critical levels.

He tried to call Katrina but, apparently, since she was in a meeting she had turned her cell phone off. He thought of, and rejected, trying to drive himself to the hospital in Oneonta as he was afraid the distraction caused by the pain would make a solo trip like that too dangerous. He tried calling the Snyder's Corners Emergency Squad but was told their only ambulance was out on a call and would probably not be back for over an hour. Jerry could not wait that long.

Then he remembered the catheter his urologist had given him for just such an emergency. Going into the bathroom, he found it in a cellophane wrapper, tucked away in his side of the medicine cabinet. Tearing the cellophane off the package, he dropped his trousers, lowered the toilet seat and sat. Slathering the catheter with K-Y jelly, he grabbed his penis with one hand and squeezed open the end of his urethra. With the other hand he attempted to insert the pointed end of the catheter into this opening. Since the catheter was made of flexible rubber, inserting it into a tight urethra was like trying to shove a greasy piece of cooked spaghetti up a flexible straw, especially where the diameter of the spaghetti was larger than that of the straw. No matter how tightly he grasped his penis, he could not get the proper leverage to thread the catheter into it. For one thing, the toilet seat was so low that his legs were above his waist making it impossible to get a straight run at the head of his penis. He needed a higher seat. This made him think of the stool he sat on to run his trains; it was high enough that he could extend his legs downward where he could get better leverage. Maybe then he could complete the job.

Kicking off his trousers so they would not impede his progress, he went downstairs to his train room. Moving the stool so it was facing the train table where he could get good light but far enough away to have ample room for his legs, he sat on the edge of the stool with his legs straight down and propped on the floor. Applying more K-Y, he again repeated the procedure he had tried upstairs. With considerable effort, this time he managed to get the catheter into the opening. Slowly, he threaded more of the catheter into his penis, giving the urethra time to stretch until, abruptly, it stopped. It was up against the swollen prostate, which was making the opening too tight for the catheter slide up and urine to run down. Jerry now pulled the catheter part way out, being careful not to allow it to come all the way out so he would have to reinsert it, covered it with more jelly and rammed it back in, twisting it as he did. At this point, the combination of the pressure on his bladder and the pain of inserting the catheter were such that he wanted it over as quickly as possible. Still twisting the catheter much like a plumber trying to open a drain with a plumbing snake, he finally managed to turn it enough to ram it past the prostate and into the bladder. Immediately urine began flowing down the inside of the catheter.

While Jerry felt instantaneous relief, this was not going to last for long.

Earlier that day he had turned on his transformer so, if they had wanted him to, he could demonstrate his layout to BoomBoom, Amy and Bill. Jerry had not remembered to turn it off. This meant there was still twenty-two volts of direct current flowing into the loop of track. In addition, Jerry had turned the stool on which he was sitting to face the layout. When the catheter breached the bladder, the urine was released in such quantity and with force that it shot out the end of the tube in an unbroken stream straight at the layout. Once this stream reached the layout track, it crossed both the outside and middle rail thus completing an electrical circuit.

Now because the amperage in an electrical train transformer is so low, even at twenty-two volts if one were to touch both the outside and middle rail, they would receive no more than a tingle since their skin would not be that good an electrical conductor. This shock would do no more that surprise the person and make him or her jump back. However, if a good electrical conductor, such as, say, a gold or silver bracelet or ring, came in contact with both rails there could be enough electricity through the conductor to cause a nasty burn to a person's skin. In Jerry's case, the urine, with an abundance of dissolved salts, was an excellent conductor.

Since the urine stream was continuous, the electrical current traveled along the stream back toward his penis, where it melted about two inches of the catheter before dissipating. An inch and a half of those two inches were inside Jerry's penis. The amount of pain was the worst than any he had felt at any time in his life.

When Katrina got home from her meeting two hours later, all she heard was a faint whimper coming from the downstairs train room. Going downstairs, she found Jerry curled into a fetal position in front of his train layout. Unable to speak as the result of nearly a solid hour of steady screaming, he could only point to his crotch. Fortunately,

Katrina was able to ascertain the problem, and immediately get Jerry, bare from the waist down, into her car for the thirty-five mile trip to the Fox Hospital emergence room.

Once there, the ER doctor took one look at Jerry's problem and immediately summoned the MedVac helicopter. Twenty minutes later, Jerry was in the operating room at Upstate Medical Center in Syracuse where a surgeon sliced open his penis and carefully scraped out the melted rubber. He then inserted a catheter into Jerry's bladder so Jerry would be able to eliminate urine and sutured him up. Later the surgeon told Katrina that the catheter would have to be taken out and reinserted on a daily basis for the next six months or until the urethra healed, whichever came first, to keep the urethra from healing shut. Jerry was going to be in pain for a long time. Somehow, this completely drove the thought of electric trains out of his mind.

****

By the time Amy and Bill were in Bill's car and on their way out of town, the road around the Stop 'N Go had been blockaded by the fire police. This necessitated a detour that added about fifteen minutes to the time it took them to get clear of Palatine County. (They had also heard the explosion and assumed, like Jerry, that it was the result of blasting in a quarry.) Once over the county line, they felt they were safe.

"I think we should go to my place in Rye." Bill was the first to break the silence. "I'm pretty sure BoomBoom won't bother us, but at any rate he doesn't know where I live and it's far enough away from North Bergen that he shouldn't be able to find us."

"Sounds like a good idea. All I know is that I'm covered with mud and need a good hot shower" Amy held out her mud-covered leg as evidence. "I have a feeling BoomBoom is too much of a coward to bother either of us. I'm just not sure how I'll face his mother at work though."

"You're probably right on the first count. The second shouldn't be a problem either. I suspect he won't bring up what happened today with her. "

Railroad (Double) Crossing: A novel

"I suppose not. From what I got talking with her, I don't even think she knows exactly what he does anyhow."

"Ok, now, what about that train?" Bill asked indicating the box lying on the seat between them.

Amy gave no answer. Rather Bill heard the window on her side open and felt a rush of cold air on his face. "There!" She said.

"You threw it out the window, didn't you?" Bill asked, not bothering to look in her direction.

"Yup."

The rest of the trip passed without any conversation but Bill was satisfied his sister had solved their problem.

****

Sheriff Pierce had just gotten home from the scene at the Stop 'N Go when the phone call came in from Becky Bisignani. Her husband had not come home from the bluestone dock and, since it was after eight, she was concerned. She had called Ray Mower who she knew worked at the dock earlier that day but Ray told her he and Jess had left early and that Tom was still there at the time. Becky wanted to know if Pierce would check for her.

When you are the Republican Sheriff in a Republican county and the wife of the Chairman of the Party asks you to do something, you do it or, come the next party caucus you would be out of a job. Therefore, Pierce hopped into his cruiser and drove out to Bisignani's Bluestone.

It was dark and the only light was the dawn to dusk light out by the loading area. The Sheriff grabbed his flashlight, got out of his car, and cursing the mud, went to the office. To his surprise, the door was half-open. *Damn,* he thought as he pushed it the rest of the way back, *I hope this isn't like one of those TV mysteries were there is someone dead in here.* To his relief, there was not. Just an empty mailing carton sitting on the table and a lot of muddy foot prints on the floor. This latter did not surprise Pierce given the mud in the yard and the fact Jess and Ray had been there earlier.

With no sign of Tom in the office, Pierce figured he would make a quick check around the yard. Since the mud had oozed into any tracks there was no indication of where those responsible for the tracks in the office had gone. Trying to ignore the mud, Bill called Tom's name a couple of times and getting no answer, slogged his way out amongst the stacks of rock. He did notice that one of the stacks had toppled over strewing loose rock in every direction. *Somebody did a piss poor job of stacking there.* he said to himself as he went by the pile. Picking his way passed the fallen pile; he stepped from rock to rock to avoid the mud as much as possible.

It was when he jumped from one big rock to the next that he noticed something white on the ground. Looking closer with his flashlight, he was able to make out that it was a white glove. Only when he tried to pick it up did he discover it had a hand in it. He was not sure, but he had an idea he had found Tom Bisignani.

Going back to the office, he used the docks phone to make a couple of calls. The first was to Ray Mower to come operate the forklift and the second to get some portable lights from the volunteer fire department. Only after Ray moved the pile of rock did Pierce know for sure who the hand belonged to. Almost completely buried in the soft mud, it took three EMT's and some shoveling, to pull the body loose.

"What you think happened?" Pierce asked Ray as they watched the EMT's bag up the body to haul it to the funeral home.

"Dunno for sure but I s'pect he might have been counting them stacks and that pile fell on him. With the weather like it has been today, that ground probably warmed up quite a bit during the day and the mud got deeper. Makes them stacks awful tippy."

"Kind of the way I figured it too. Damn tough way to go though, crushed like that. Well, thanks for your help, Ray, guess I gotta go tell Mrs. Bisignani that she's a widow. "

"Ok, I'll put the forklift away and be getting out of here too." Ray nodded as the Sheriff went back to his cruiser. "Beginning to feel a might nippy too."

"Yup. Channel Four's AccuWeather gal says that low is starting to move and there'll be a cold front coming in. May only get up into the twenties tomorrow. Snow, too, by midweek." Price shut the cruiser's door and, with mud slapping at the bottom of the fenders, pulled out on Route 618 heading toward the Bisignani house.

— Epilogue —

KEVIN SHEPARD HAD THE week off from school for Presidents' Week and, despite what was probably going to be only one or two of the few nice days of his vacation, had spent the first day off playing computer games. Only because his mother wanted a little time with his Uncle Dave, was Kevin sent out of their doublewide and told to either do something outside or go over to Peter's. (Although Kevin was only ten, he was smart enough to know uncles were supposed to be blood related and they did not share beds with aunts that were not their wives. Not only that, but this was the third "uncle" that had stayed with them in the last year.) Since there was nothing outside that he was interested in doing, Kevin started down the road toward Peter's house. It was when he reached the end of his driveway that he spotted the box sticking out of what was left of a big snow bank.

At first, he thought the white, blue and orange box was just a piece of garbage that some slob, not wanting it to clutter up their car, had tossed it out along the road. But when he went over to it and gave it a kick he was surprised that it was heavier than an empty box should have been. As it rolled over Kevin could see there was something inside it. Only when he picked it up did he see that the contents were a toy train engine and car.

Now Kevin, being born in the late nineteen nineties, not only had never seen a steam engine but also was completely unaware of the existence of such things as O-gauge, electric trains. When he looked at what was in the box, he had no idea what it was or how it operated. Interested, he put the box under his arm and continued this trip down the road to Peter's house.

Fortunately for both Kevin's and Peter's education, Peter's dad was on seasonal unemployment—he drove a grader for the county and worked only during the summer—and happened to be home that afternoon. The reason this was fortunate was that Peter's dad, Bob Howard, actually not only knew what electric trains were but also had an old Marx set in a box someplace in the cellar. He told the kids that if they could find it, there was a transformer there and they could use it, along with the track in the same box, to run the train Kevin had found. Assuming it would run.

Always looking for something new to do, the boys went on a treasure hunt in the Howard's cellar and, after a forty-five minute search, came up with the box holding Bob's train set. With Bob giving instructions, the boys were able to set up an oval of track on the living room floor and attach the transformer to it. In order to be sure of correct wheel alignment, Bob took it upon himself to place the locomotive and tender on the tracks to so the locomotive's wheels would not get crosswise to the middle and outside rail and short it out. Once he was certain that the train was on the tracks correctly he told Peter to move the transformer handle forward to power up the track.

Before he started, Peter had only one question. "What", he wanted to know, "does New York Central stand for?"

Bob said that he had no idea.

Then, as Peter slowly moved the handle forward, first the headlights on the Hudson began to glow, getting brighter as he applied more power. Just when the lights reached their brightest, the drive wheels on the locomotive began to turn and the train started to move. Peter gave more power and the train's wheels moved faster, until it was fairly flying around the track. The drive rods were a blur. On his dad's advice, Peter pushed the button on the transformer labeled whistle and it caused an ear splitting sound. Both boys hooted in delight. Next, he pushed the bell button and the train's bell began dinging until he pushed it again.

Together, Kevin and Peter giggled in delight as the locomotive and its tender sped around the track, swaying from side to side and then rocking up on the outer wheels as it went around the tight curves. Finally, the force of inertia being too great, it fell off the track. Undaunted, they picked it up and tried to get it realigned without shutting off the power from the transformer. This caused an electrical fizz and down in the cellar, a breaker to trip. There was also the distinctive smell of ozone in the air.

After Bob went down and reset the breaker, he showed the boys the correct way to align the train's wheels and they powered up again. This time, nothing happened. The train sat there. Its lights did not come on. Somehow, the power surge caused by either the derailment or their misalignment had burned out something inside the locomotive. Eager to correct the mistake, and not immediately willing to accept Bob's verdict that in less than five minutes of operation they had ruined the locomotive, the boys took the locomotive down to Bob's workbench and, after locating the screws that held it together, opened it. Once inside, however, they were stymied since there was not a circuit board in sight, just a few wires leading from the pickup rollers to the motor. Not seeing anything loose or burned, they had no idea what to do next, so, at Peter's suggestion, they left the two pieces of locomotive on the bench and went to Peter's room to get on an Internet chat where they probably were talking either to a pervert or a police officer posing as one..

Two days later, and after a lot of nagging by his mother, Peter finally took the tracks apart and returned them and the transformer to the box in the cellar. Seeing the unassembled locomotive sitting on his dad's workbench, and before being scolded for leaving it there, he attached the tender to it and tossed both into the trash box next to the door. Early that afternoon, Bob, having nothing better to do and wanting to get rid of the trash before the impending snowstorm made travel impossible, carried the trash box out to his car. Later, on his way into town, he tossed the contents of the box into the ravine that served the neighborhood as a dump.

The locomotive, in two pieces and with the tender attached, bounced off an outdated black and white television set and landed at the bottom of the ravine along with the discarded refuse of several families. There it finally came to rest on the edge of a stream whose water, at that exact minute, would eventually end up in the glass of a tenant on the lower Eastside of New York City. The snowstorm had started and the heavy, wet snow took only a matter of seconds to completely cover the Hudson and its tender with a white blanket, soon making it invisible.

— An Afterword —

SHERIFF BILL PIERCE HAD a message from **Steve Gates**, director of Gates and Son Funeral Home, waiting for him when he came into his office on Tuesday morning. The message was brief: "Get over here ASAP." As soon as Pierce walked into the home, Gates handed him a mud encrusted pistol he had found when cleaning up **Tom Bisignani's** body. Gates also informed the Sheriff that the gun was loaded, as the .22 caliber handgun had gone off and the bullet had just missed his assistant while they were trying to hose the mud off the body. Apparently, the force and weight of the falling rock had embedded the pistol in Bisignani's chest until the water pressure from the hose dislodged it.

Pierce thanked the director and took the gun back to his office where he ran the serial number through Bureau of Criminal Investigation's data bank. It turned out that the pistol, along with several other handguns and rifles, had been stolen in a burglary at a sporting goods store in upper Pennsylvania about three years ago. Bob could not help but wonder how Tom had come to own it and why he was carrying it in his bluestone dock last night. For one thing, it was a lady's gun and for another, it was not something that would be very effective in warding off thieves. Bob thought that it might have been that Tom was going to use it to shoot rats.

Not much for pondering, Bob tossed the pistol into the drawer of his desk for safekeeping. A stolen handgun that no one knew you had was a handy thing for a police officer to have available just in case it ever became necessary to plant it on a perp.

Other than the gun, he had no further interest in how Tom came to be buried in the mud under the pile of rock. He left that to OSHA to figure out. Their investigators in turn ruled it an industrial accident and suggested that, in the future, rock pallets be only stacked two high. That officially closed the case as far as both the Sheriff and government were concerned.

****

Becky Bisignani made a discovery of her own. In the process of clearing up Tom's business, she found some disturbing things on both his personal and business computers. She made the first discovery on the computer in Tom's home office when she clicked on a file that was headed **dutchstone**, thinking it might have something to do with his business. Instead, pictures of preteen girls posed in frontal nudity popped up on the screen as well as several links to Internet sites containing child porn. Horrified, she tried a couple more files, which Tom had labeled **thaistone, namstone** and **swedestone**; all were the same kind of thing. Some contained pictures of girls, others of boys; some had girls and boys together; all had links to similar porn sites. On every web site, the children shown had not reached or just barely reached, puberty. Disgusted, she deleted these files and their links as best she could. She was also aware that they would still be, somehow, embedded on the hard drive. Moreover, she was not sure how many others of the files contained like kinds of things under equally innocent titles. So she made a mental note to trash the computer. She was also afraid to do this in the county landfill since she was aware that there were people who "picked the dump" and could possibly recover this information. She would have to dump it in some out-of-the-way spot.

Later that day, while checking Tom's business computer in the dock's office, she found the same files on it and deleted them. She then loaded this second computer into her car to take it home with her. Also while cleaning out his office she found a cardboard mailing box on the office floor addressed to William Lawyer and sent from Lionel. Not knowing why it was there but suspecting it might be important to someone, she brought it home and tossed it, along with a well-thumbed copy of Lolita she found under the couch in the train room, into the burn-barrel. The next day, after carefully checking to make sure she was not being watch, she tossed both of the computers into a deep ravine along a back road between Snyder's Corners and Ferrioville.

As far as Tom's train collection was concerned, while leafing through his latest issue of O-Gauge RailRoading magazine, she found a full-page ad for buyer who specialized in selling model railroading items. Contacting him by phone, he immediately sent an appraiser who lowballed the price on all of Tom's items. However, even at fifty cents on the dollar of what the items were worth, Becky received a huge amount of cash for Tom's collection of trains, accessories and paper products. Enough, in fact, that after disposing of the collection, Tom's bluestone dock along with the inventory and selling the Bisignani homestead that had been in the family for almost two centuries, she had a sizable inheritance. This fortune enabled her to get out of the "God forsaken" Palatine county and buy a condo in a retirement community in Florida's Panhandle near Destin.

Here she met a nice, much older, retired widower who, when she asked, said, much to her relief, that he knew absolutely nothing about model trains. After a short courtship, they were married and lived in his condominium until his death a year later. Now with a second inheritance, Becky decided she wanted to travel the world and had the money to do it. While scuba diving over the Australian Great Barrier Reef, she was attacked and eaten by a huge Great White shark.

****

Two high school students, while out squirrel hunting came upon two computers in a ravine along an unmarked county road. Lugging them back home, they discovered both machines, although dinged up a bit, were usable. The boys reconfigured them to play computer games.

Neither boy ever became aware that there was child porn etched onto the hard drives.

****

Jeremiah VanVierden's penis took the full six months to heal fully. When he came to after the operation to remove the pieces of the catheter, Katrina told him about the Sheriff finding Tom's body. Like everyone else, Jerry assumed Tom's death was just an unfortunate accident. Because she did not think it was important, Katrina never told him about the explosion at the Stop 'N Go. Once he got home the debris had been cleared, the convenience store restored and, because the victim was from out-of-state, the story was no longer news. Consequently he was never aware of what happened to BoomBoom. This was fortunate since Jerry was the only one who could have put the pieces together and connected Tom, BoomBoom, Bill and Amy. Luckily for all involved as the result of the trauma from the Acute Urine Retention and the subsequent operation, most of that morning's meeting and the reasons for it had been repressed in his memory. Even the train set was no longer important to him.

After he had recovered from his operation, his urologist, checking Jerry's PSA numbers, found them elevated so he preformed another biopsy. This time, perhaps triggered by the trauma of that Monday in February or just the Law of Averages, the biopsy turned up a couple of cancer cells in one sample so, at the doctor's suggestion, Jerry had the gland surgically removed. This, at least, put an end to his AUR worry. It also necessitated that Jerry be on a catheter again for another four months. During his recuperation time from both operations, Jerry completely lost interest in his trains and, while recovering from the second surgery, boxed them up and sold them through eBay at a considerable loss. Just the act of getting rid of them was therapeutic.

Once he had fully recovered from the loss of the prostate and subsequent rehab, he took up golf with a vengeance. This at least gave him and Katrina something they could still do together. Spending most of the money that he realized from the sale of his trains, he bought the most expensive set of golf clubs he could afford and took lessons from the teaching pros at both the Kaaterskill Country Club and a course near his winter home in San Juan. Since the advice from two different teachers conflicted in many areas, these lessons only confused him to the point where, whenever he addressed the ball, his mind filled with so much clutter that it was a surprise he could even swing the club. Thus conflicted, he occasionally had good holes and a few decent enough rounds to keep him coming back but Jerry was only able to break one hundred once in his life.

It occurred on the San Juan course three years later. Jerry needed a twenty-foot putt for a par on the eighteenth hole for a ninety-nine. When the ball toppled into the hole, Jerry tossed his putter high in the air, jumped around, and hugged Katrina, who, along with another couple, witnessed the act. The club, obeying the Laws of Gravity, fell straight down, with the putter's head coming first. Inasmuch as Jerry was using a heavy mallet-type putter, the weight was considerable so when it hit him on the head, he suffered a massive concussion. He fell onto the green and died when a clot from the brain hemorrhage floated into his slightly constricted coronary artery and blocked it. He might have survived had clubhouse attendants been able to use the club's defibrillator but the directions were written in English and they were literate only in Spanish.

Because Jerry's death was unattended the San Juan medical examiner was required to do an autopsy of his body. During the examination the doctor found not only the blocked artery but that Jerry had stage-two liver, bladder and pancreatic cancer. It was surmised that the cause of these were prostrate cancer cells that had been loosened and entered the blood stream during either of his two biopsies or the removal surgery. The medical examiner told Katrina that if the putter had not killed her husband, Jerry would have been dead within a year from any of those cancers.

****

The following spring, a task force of State Police and Otsego County Sheriff's deputies raided **Madame Orey**'s Massage Parlor. They charged the Madame, whose real name was Mary Alger, with soliciting for the purpose of performing acts of prostitution. Before her trial could commence, however, she hinted that her client list included many prominent politicians in both Otsego and Palatine counties. The DA, seeing retreat was a better form of valor, reduced the charge to dispensing medical advice without a license, a misdemeanor, and let Ms Alger off with a small fine. She moved out of the area and set up shop in Miami where there were elderly male retirees that could use her services.

****

Nick Mower and **Jess Felton** combined their assets and bought Tom Bisignani's bluestone dock from his widow. The renamed it Palatine Stone and using their combined skill at working with stone, were able to keep it going as an important player in the building and field stone market. Eventually, they hired **Bob Howard** as a full-time forklift operator.

****

Peter Potts finally, after some litigation, received payment from the new owners of Palatine Stone for the pallets he had delivered to Bisignani Bluestone. Since the suit caused a lot of animosity between him and Nick and Jess, Peter decided he had had enough of the rock collecting business. Using the money from the stone and the sale of one of his Bobcats and truck as well as the natural gas leases for his property, he purchased a small herd of Hereford cattle. Since it had been more than seven years since he had last used any artificial fertilizers—or any fertilizers for that matter—on his farm, he easily qualified for organic farming status. This allowed him to sell grass-fed, organic beef at inflated prices with almost no work on his part. All that was required was to pasture the cattle during the summer and harvest enough hay to keep their weight up over the winter. Since the hay was stored in large, round, plastic covered, bales, it was not necessary to even store it in the barn or to feed every day. Using his remaining Bobcat, all he needed to do was forklift a bale from the edge of the hayfield into the pasture a couple of times a week and pull off the plastic cover. He was now free to stay away from the cows as much as possible. Then too, about the time he reached the point where the cattle were getting to him, he just sent most of them to be slaughtered.

****

Bill Farmer continued to work as a volunteer at the Toy Train Museum in Strasburg. The following spring, while digging around in a box of odds in ends in the Silver Hall at York, he came upon a shell for a Lionel Hudson. Thinking it might be from the 1929 model, he bought it for a dollar and took it home, where, once cleaned up, it became a prominate part of his collection.

****

As a grieving mother, **Clare Cleary** had to put up with the ordeal of having a Channel 4 Action News Team stick a camera and microphone in her face, while she answered questions about her son and his death in the explosion. She tried to do the best job she could. Considering the circumstances, she was relieved when everyone at the diner the next day told her that she carried it off very well. This made it worthwhile to her.

Since there was very little of Sean left for her to bury, the funeral was brief and not especially costly. The day after the interment, a lawyer, who managed to get her number from the funeral home, called her with an offer to help her sue the Stop 'N Go Corporation for negligence in the death of her son. The case, settled out of court for a half-million dollars, fifty-five percent of which came to Clare, gave her enough money so she was finally able to quit her job at the diner. In addition, she was also able to sell all the merchandise from her garage and Sean's apartment on eBay for another five thousand dollars. Using this nest egg for retirement, she left North Bergen and bought a one-bedroom mobile home in a retirement complex just outside Miami Beach. Once settled in, she bought two toy poodles, a female and male, which she named Amy and Nick. She never again sold anything on eBay but spent the remainder of her life having her hair dyed various shades of lavender and indulging her dogs. She died five years later of complications from emphysema.

****

Amy Weaver—she went back to her maiden name—not willing to face Clare again, quit her job at the diner via a phone call the next day. After a few weeks and since no one ever questioned her or Bill about Tom's death, she relaxed. Thus freed up by quitting her job, she used this time to locate a collector who was willing to buy the display Barbie for two thousand dollars and the others for five hundred dollars each. Using this money plus the rest of what she inherited from her uncle's estate, she was able to afford analysis. Here she finally came to terms with her sexual self-esteem and feelings toward her parents. This allowed her to reconcile with her mother. After her father died, she helped her mother move into an assisted living facility just outside of Rhinebeck. Amy always managed to visit her three times a year: Mother's Day, Christmas and on her mother's birthday.

That February fifteenth was not the last time Amy was in Snyder's Corners. She went back one more time. Because she was required to sign the papers when they sold the store, she reluctantly went along with Bill. Maybe because she no longer had to worry about running into Tom or possibly due to the progress she was making in therapy, this trip turned our entirely differently from the previous ones.

After they had signed the papers, **Sam Aaronson** asked if she and Bill would like to join him for a drink at the Tavern next door. After a couple of drinks and a hamburgers for dinner, both she and Sam were having such a good time and seeming to hit it off so well that he asked if he could see her again. She accepted. (**John Givens** was out of her life by this time. He had been arrested as an illegal alien and deported back to Jamaica). The date, a Broadway play and candlelight dinner, led to others, and a year later Sam proposed. Amy said that she would accept under only one condition; that she did not have to live in Snyder's Corners. This was fine with Sam, who opened up a branch office of Aaronson, Aaronson and Bernstein in Poughkeepsie.

Once married, Amy and Sam bought an old house overlooking what was once the mainline tracks of the NY Central on the eastern bank of the Hudson River. Amy immediately made plans to enroll at Marist College and get her degree in fine arts with the intention of opening a small gallery in New York City. There was one tiny roadblock to this idea, however. Nine months after the wedding and after an especially difficult pregnancy, Amy delivered a healthy baby boy. She did not name him William.

****

William Weaver, likewise freed from worry about either Tom or BoomBoom, taught right up to his fifty-fifth birthday, celebrated it, and retired. Having sold the toy trucks and Ken dolls to the same collector his sister sold the Barbies to, he invested this money along with the twenty-five thousand in cash and his part of the sale of the store in Snyder's Corners. These investments along with his New York State Teachers' Retirement, assured that he would have enough for a very comfortable retirement. In fact, he was so happy; he even gave **John Carson** one of the G.I. Joes for his help. He left teaching with no regrets and without ever looking back.

Also feeling flush with this extra money gave him more confidence in other parts of his life. For one thing, he overcame his fear about negotiating New York City's freeways enough to purchase a small cottage out on Long Island at Montauk. This gave him a place to spend his free time with **Mildred Kline** after they resumed their relationship. While neither was interested in taking this relationship to the next level, they thoroughly enjoyed each others company and would remain together for a long time.

Since by the time Amy remarried, their father had died, it was Bill's job to give her away when she married Sam. A year later, he began a career of the favorite uncle after her son was born. Knowing she was in therapy and seeing the progress she had made with their mother, he never mentioned the thing with Uncle William or Tom again. He also could not help but notice that her jaw line no longer had the hard set to it, apparently the death of Bisignani plus marriage and motherhood had changed her outlook on life.

At Mildred's urging and with her help, Bill entered the Computer Age and purchased a HP laptop. This allowed him to establish contact with his daughter, Chloe. In so doing, he underwent his own form of therapy first by long distance—they emailed back and forth on the Internet—and then in person when she asked him to come to Seattle to visit her. By this time, happily married, she had given birth to a son. When Bill first met him, the boy was five. The connection between grandpa and grandson was immediate.

The following summer, just before his second visit to Seattle, Bill and Mildred happened to be taking a detour along Merrick Road through Freeport on their way back from a weekend in Montauk. Bill spotted a hobby shop and, on a whim, stopped the car. Going into the shop he discovered, among other things, that they sold electric toy trains. For no particular reason except that he wanted something to enjoy with his grandson, Bill bought a MTH starter set that the owner of the shop recommended as a good way to go. He had the set shipped to his daughter with orders to wait until his visit to open it. When Bill arrived a week later, he and his grandson had a ball setting up and playing with the set. With the train circling the track, his grandson blowing the whistle and ringing the bell, Bill knew he could never be happier in his life than he was right at that minute.

— Words to the Readers —

ASIDE FOR ANY HISTORIC figures all persons in this novel are fictional creations of the author and not a portrayal of anyone, living or dead. That does not mean there are not certain characteristics that are found in real people, it just means there is no one, as far as I know, with all those characteristics in the same combination of personality traits.

Likewise Palatine County and Snyder's Corners do not exist as particular localities but are fictional compositions of a variety of locations in upstate New York. If one were to examine the area delineated by the Thruway on the North, Hudson River on the East, NY Route 17/ Interstate 86 (aka The Quickway) on the South and the Finger Lakes on the West, they would find areas and places that fit the description of the county and city meteorologically, politically and economically. Having spent the majority of my life as well as having ancestral stock in this area I can attest to the fact that it does exists.

Please note: **Z-4000, Digital Command System (DCS)** and **Protosound©** are products of MTH Electric Trains, 7020 Columbia Gateway Dr., Columbia, MD 21046. Likewise, **Train Master Command Control (TMCC)** is the product of Lionel LLC, 26750 23 Mile Rd. Chesterfield, MI 48051. Since the writing of this novel MTH has gone into their third version of **DCS** while Lionel is offering a new control system call **Legacy**. Both systems continue to have their fans and detractors.

Before you go searching your attic or basement for a Lionel, NYC Hudson, #LN131928, be aware that it is a completely fictional model. In fact, a model like this may well have been beyond the manufacturing capabilities of Lionel or any toy train manufacturer in 1929 but I needed to create a desirable model that would be able to operate on some of today's equipment. This does not, however, mean there are not specific models out there that are as sophisticated and/or more desired by collectors. Many are worth as much or more to the right person as the one I created for this story. Whether someone would be willing to murder one or more people to obtain the model is something I cannot say for sure but knowing the obsession of some members of TCA, I would not completely rule it out.

As far as the conflict between MTH and Lionel, there has not been any attempt on my part to do anything more than repeat the rumor and innuendo that floated around the hobby during the ten years or so between latter part of the last century and the first part of this. This disinformation was circulated primarily through postings on the Internet. By way of disclosure, I have met Mike Wolf on a number of occasions and found him to be a great person whose only interest seems to be in producing toy trains that look and operate as close to the real thing as possible. The fact that he was demonized by the Louies is very similar to what happened to Abe Lincoln during the Civil War. It would seem there were people on both sides of the Moonie/Louie conflict that claim to know the truth and were more than willing to spread their version of it while ridiculing the other side's story. As in any civil war the truth is what each side believes it to be, regardless of any facts to the contrary. However, as I have noted, at the extremes there is real animosity between the two camps, especially over the law suit, the judgment of which sent Lionel into bankruptcy, apparently, as a means to protect itself.

However, by 2008 and after the timeline for this novel, Lionel and MTH had settled their differences and, in fact, joined forces for the betterment of the hobby. After Lionel emerged from bankruptcy, MTH signed an agreement with them to produce replicas of their tinplate trains. By 2009 MTH was offering locomotives, rolling stock, and accessories based on prewar Lionel designs. It should be noted that these locos are run using **DCS.**

I also must confess to owning a lot of MTH stock and running my layout using **DCS**. If this makes me a Moonie, so be it. Like Jeremiah, I happened to have started my main collection just as **DCS** was making its entry into the field of toy trains and stuck with it. I do not, however, have any strong feelings in regard to Lionel and own a lot of their accessories as well as items produced by a number of other manufacturers. They all have built some great stuff, particularly in the latter part of the twentieth century and into the twenty-first.

If you are interested in toy trains, especially of the O-gauge variety I would highly recommend subscribing to <u>O-Gauge Railroading Magazine</u> at 33 Sheridan Rd, Youngstown OH 44514-9979. The magazine, published 7 times a year, is loaded with valuable information that will get you started or keep you in the hobby. Likewise, if you have any questions, problems, or comments about O-gauge trains, either buying or running, the best source for help is their O-Gauge Forum operated by the publisher at <u>www.ogaugerr.com</u>. The information is free—you do not even have to subscribe to the magazine—and the hobbyists that post there are very knowledgeable. Not only will they fill you in on everything from operating systems to the latest rumors in the hobby, but you will make some great friends. The Forum is also a good place to learn about nearby train shops and clubs.

On the other hand, if you are serious about getting into toy trains, especially O-gauge, you should consider joining Train Collectors Association, if, for no other reason, to gain admittance to the York meet. As pointed out above, one needs to have two sponsors, which can easily be gotten either at your local train club or through O-Gauge's Forum. The address is TCA, P.O. Box 248, Strasburg PA 17579-0248 for an application or you can check them out online at <u>www.traincollectors.org</u> . Be warned, this is an organization for serious toy train people and, while membership can be worth every penny to the serious hobbyist, it can get expensive.

Finally, toy trains can be one of the greatest hobbies for an adult and child to share. I strongly recommend it to anyone with the least bit of interest. You will never regret it.

Jim Mortensen

TCA #02-54464

Oxford, NY

November, 2009